KATIE

Graham Duncanson

ISBN: 978-0-244-02638-7

Also by this author

Mating Lions

Fiona

Francesca

Anna

Chapter 1

The promise of a real safari

Katie slumped down in a chair by a table outside the famous 'Thorn Tree'. This was part of the five star hotel, 'The New Stanley', in Nairobi. She pulled her small wheeled cabin crew suitcase near to her, if that got stolen, that would be the last straw. She was hot, although it was still only mid-morning. She was in full BOAC uniform. She longed to take her stockings off. She ordered a coffee from a hovering waiter. She could not stop herself; a tear ran down her face, smudging her make up. What was she to do now? One thing for certain she was not going to return to the 'Panafric Hotel' and be laughed at by the rest of the crew. In her misery she did not notice the man, until he was right in front of her. He didn't look well, as he said,

"May I join you? I feel my head is going to explode. You look even more miserable than I feel. Beautiful girls like you are very rare in Kenya. You mustn't cry." Another tear ran down her face as she replied,

"You must be ill. I know that I look a complete mess and I'm not beautiful at all. Do join me. I have ordered a coffee. I'm sure the waiter will get another one for you, when he arrives with mine. I imagine your headache is self inflicted?"

"Yes. It was my thirtieth birthday last night and I had a skin full. I have just picked up some vaccine and stores. I have got to drive one hundred and seventy miles up into the NFD and I don't think I can face it." Her coffee arrived and she ordered one for him. He just sat with his head in his hands. The effort of talking seemed to have been the last nail in his coffin. Katie did not know why she said,

"I'm not doing anything. I could drive you." Was it his lovely sad brown eyes or was it because she was a kind loving girl and felt sorry for him? He looked up and said,

"Surely you are about to fly somewhere? You are all dressed in your uniform."

"It is a long story, so I won't bore you with it, but somehow I have managed to be stuck here for a week on my own. Where is the NFD?"

"It stands for the Northern Frontier District. It is the hot dry country stretching north from Mount Kenya to the Ethiopian border."

"So you are going on safari?"

"Yes, you could certainly say that. It is going to be a real safari not one of these minibus trips round game lodges."

Katie then made her mind up. If she hadn't made such a fool of herself last night, she had been about to go on safari that morning, just as he described in a minibus. She stood up and said,

"Come on. I want to go on a real safari. I will drive you. Where is your car?" The man looked at her with some amazement and pointed to a long wheel-base Landrover with a substantial roof rack. He paid the waiter for their coffees, picked up her bag and led her to the vehicle. He opened the back door and put in her case. Katie said,

"Can you shield me? I can't stand another second in these stockings."

She used him and the back door as a shield. She hitched up skirt and gave him a wonderful view of her thighs, as she unbuttoned her stockings from her suspender-belt.

He held the driver's door open for her. Girls in relatively tight skirts are not meant to get into Landrovers which are quite high up. He got a view of her skin coloured knickers and thought for a second that she wasn't wearing any. He had temporarily forgotten about his headache. He went around to the other door and got in. She appeared to know what she was doing, as she had already started the vehicle. He just said,

"You are being a real angel. Straight on and go left at the lights. I'm Ian Richardson." Katie did not look at him but said,

"I'm Katie Kent."

Ian guided her though the traffic in Nairobi and soon they were on the Thika road. He asked,

"Do you like pineapples?"

"Yes, I love them."

"Just pull in near those chaps." There was a quick conversation in Swahili. Ian reached into the small compartment between the instrument panel and the steering-wheel. He gave an African two coins and was given a large pineapple. He put it behind them in a cardboard box, as she drew off. He said,

"I feel pretty dreadful. Do you mind if I have a nap? We are going to Nanuyki and then on to Isiolo."

Ian then pulled a pillow from the back and having put his head on it, was almost instantly asleep.

Katie thought, '*What have I let myself in for? Well at least I won't see any of the crew again for a week.* She let her blond hair out of its bun and enjoyed the sense of freedom. She added to this by shrugging out of her uniform jacket and undoing her cravat. For good measure she undid the top three buttons of her blouse.

She mused, as she drove the Landrover with some panache, *'You can take a farmer's daughter out of Norfolk but you can't take Norfolk out of her'*. She was happy again.

Katie did well with her navigating, but she did overshoot the turning, signed to Nyeri and Nanuyki, at Fort Hall. She turned around. Ian who was still dead to the world, flopped, so that his head was in her lap. She tried to push him back up, but she wasn't strong enough and in his sleep he just snuggled down to make himself more comfortable. Her skirt, as she had been driving, had ridden up, so now his chin which was covered in stubble was rubbing on her thigh. She thought, '*Bloody hell, because I haven't got a tan and just got slightly burnt, sunbathing yesterday, I'm going to get a rash.'* She giggled. '*That will take some explaining!'*

Then she smiled as she remembered with some pleasure that she would not be seeing the others for a week. Ian moved again, but she was too busy looking at the sign showing her that she had to keep right on to Nanuyki rather than turn left to Nyeri, to bother with him. When she looked down he had his face buried in her crutch. She knew enough about sex to know that anyone looking through the window would have a fit to see where his face was, but she could not be concerned.' She laughed.

Ian woke with a start, as they we're entering Nanuyki. When he found where his face was he was mortified.

"I'm so sorry. You poor girl!"

“Don't worry you promised me a really rough safari. Your chin has not let you down. Thank goodness my skirt is quite long so no one will see my rash!” She lifted her skirt so Ian could see a lightly tanned thigh with a bright red rash.

“Oh my goodness, I didn't realise a girl’s thighs were so sensitive. I didn't shave this morning.” Katie giggled,

“If you think that if you shave tomorrow, you can put your face there again. You have got another think coming!”

They filled up with petrol in Nanuyki. Katie found the temperature was rather good. It was roughly the same as a warm summer’s day in England. She didn't feel such an idiot in her air hostess uniform. As they set off North for Timau, Ian who was obviously feeling better volunteered to take over the driving. After ten miles the Tarmac stopped and they were on a dusty marram road. Katie was feeling sleepy. She said to Ian,

“Is anyone likely to look in the window?”

“Not a chance we are just about to drop down into the hot country.”

She made herself comfortable with her head in his lap. He smiled. Ian certainly felt better from his hangover and he could see the change in Katie. She seemed so much happier. He wondered what had happened to her the previous night which had made her so miserable. He thought,’ *I'm sure she will tell me when she is ready.’*

She did not wake until they stopped at the Police barrier in Isiolo. Ian had a joke with the Policemen. They lifted the barrier and then they got going. Katie sat up with a groan,

“Christ, it's hot.”

“I had noticed that you had stripped off a bit, but that you were not very suitably dressed for the NFD!”

“What do other girls wear in the NFD?” Ian looked rather shamed faced and said,

“Actually I have never taken a girl up into the NFD. I certainly have not taken any girl anywhere as glamorous as you.”

Katie looked down at her filthy blouse and the sweat running down her chest which had made dust streaks. She laughed.

“You are a complete bugger. You persuaded me to drive you and you have never brought a girl here before!”

"Well it is rather wild country and you did not seem to need much persuading. You seemed to want to get out of Nairobi as quickly as possible and so coming with me seemed to suit both of us. I'm sorry if I mislead you. One thing for sure is, when you talk to chums back in the UK who have been to Kenya, they may have been to Masailand or Tsavo, but the farthest North anyone will have gone would be Samburu which we are going by, as we speak, and we have only just started our safari."

"I suppose I will have to forgive you, as I was pretty desperate this morning."

"If you will forgive me for asking, what had happened to you last night which made you so unhappy?"

Katie poured her heart out to him. She told him, she was a farmer's daughter and she had always wanted to be an air hostess. She had been accepted by BOAC on their training scheme when she was eighteen. She had done well and had been taken into the 'Long Haul' branch. This was her first overseas flight. Because of the schedules they had been given an extended stop-over in Kenya of seven days. The plan was that all the crew would go on a fairly up-market safari in two mini buses, after their first night at the 'Panafric Hotel'.

They had all been booked in. The airline always paid for them to have separate rooms. They all went to bed after a fairly lively supper with quite a large amount of alcohol being drunk. At the meal the Senior Captain, called Algernon, sat next to Katie. Katie said he was very chatty. However after he had drunk quite a bit, he put his hand rather far up her thigh. She had firmly removed it. After another half hour he tried it again. Katie had difficulty removing it without causing a scene. She said she was relived when the meal was over. When she was getting ready to go to bed and was in her pyjamas, there was a knock on her door. She naively had opened the door thinking it was one of the other girls. The Captain had barged in. He had grabbed at her after he had locked the door. She had hit him hard on his shoulder with the bedside light and then screamed at him, saying if he didn't get out she would really scream the place down. She was still holding the lamp when he left. In the morning at breakfast the head air hostess, called Yvonne, told her that the Captain requested that she was not invited on the safari, as she was too young. One of the other girls had taunted her by saying that obviously she had not delivered the goods last night! So Katie had packed up her stuff and walked down to the 'New Stanley', where Ian had met her.

Ian turned quickly and saw she was crying again. He regretted asking her.

"Poor you, I did not mean to upset you." She replied,

"I'm glad I told you. I feel better having told some one. I am sure I will be moved off 'Long Haul' when I get back to London. I am bloody miserable now. I certainly don't want to work for BOAC. I'm sure the word will get round that I'm frigid and I can't deliver the goods!" Ian replied,

"I think you did bloody well fighting him off." Katie blew her nose and replied,

"I glad I didn't loose my virginity to that bastard!"

They drove on in silence. Then Ian said,

"Shall we turn round? I hate to think of you being terrified out of your wits being all alone with me out in the bush. We could get back to Nanuyki Sports Club where I am a member. They have a nice pool and you could have a room to yourself." Katie replied,

"Certainly not, I said that I was coming on a rough safari with you and that's what I'll do. Somehow I totally trust you. Why I can't imagine, as you have spent the afternoon with your face in my crutch!"

"I'm so sorry it was so crass of me." Ian reached out and squeezed her hand. Katie laughed,

"I'm not sure squeezing my hand was very reassuring! However I took it to mean. I will look after you, rather than, at the first opportunity my hand will be in your knickers!"

"Katie, you have a lovely turn of phrase. I will look after you."

After another half an hour, Ian turned off the road down a fairly well used track, telling her that in a couple of hundred yards they would reach a good camping spot, where he had camped before under some big trees.

It was a beautiful campsite, lots of shade under the trees and no bush. There was soft sand under foot. However Ian told Katie to keep her shoes on, as there would be thorns about. Katie smiled because Ian was obviously really used to setting up his camp on his own, but there were no plans for anyone else. He tried really hard. Katie just wanted to help, but didn't know what to do. A camp table was set up and a chair put beside it. Ian said,

"You must be knackered, have a seat."

So Katie sat down and felt like visiting royalty. A kettle was filled and put on a small gas stove. A mug and a pewter tankard were found. Katie realised that everything was just for one.

She also realised, what Ian had meant about turning around and going to a club. Obviously there was only one tent but more importantly there was probably only one bed. Katie could not analyse her feelings. '*Was she terrified? She had never shared a bed with a man, or was a tiny part of her slightly excited. Why was the Senior Captain so horrible and slimy, yet Ian who was twelve years her senior was not*?' The kettle whistled and halted her thoughts. At least she could make the tea. Ian had put a tin of tea bags on the table.

He had heard the whistle. He ran back with an armful of dry wood. Katie called,

"Don't run. I have tea covered. Please give me jobs to do."

"If you could be in charge of tea and then three-quarters fill the big metal bucket with water that would be great. I will get the fire going to heat the water for our shower and also to use for cooking. That little gas stove is really only any good for boiling the kettle." Katie thought, '*A shower will be good. Bloody hell will I be expected to have it in the nude? I suppose I can shower in my bikini. At least I have got one of those. Otherwise I have brought totally the wrong clothes. I'm such an idiot bringing a suspender-belt. Well I suppose I just brought all I had.'*

The fire was soon going with the bucket next to it, together with a grill on legs. Tea was drunk, as they continued doing other things. Katie wrapped potatoes in tin foil and made a salad with lettuce, cucumber and tomatoes. Then she prepared the pineapple. Ian got the tent erected on the roof of the Landrover and the shower which consisted of a canvass bag with a rose under it, hoisted into a tree, under which were a canvass bath and a ground sheet. There was also a canvass basin on a wooden stand. Katie casually asked about a loo. She was told sadly that there was not one available, but there was a '*panga*' (machete), a box of matches and a loo-roll. Ian caused her slight alarm by saying that you dug a hole, did your business, wiped your bottom, burnt the paper and then filled in the hole. He said it was best not to go too far, as he had seen lion and leopard in this area. Katie consoled herself by thinking, '*perhaps being eaten by a lion was preferable to being sexually assaulted by the Aircraft Captain*'.

Supper was put on as the tropical darkness rapidly descended. Katie thought the timing would be all wrong, as the potatoes were put in the fire at the same time as the sausages were put on the grill. She was wrong. The potatoes seemed to cook amazingly fast. She was given a beer in the rinsed out tankard. Ian drank his out of the bottle. It was lovely and cold, as he had a cold box, on which he put one of the seats of the Landrover, to make a second chair. A gas light was lit. Without thinking Katie hitched up her skirt to look at her rash and said,

"My thighs are not as delicate as I thought. Look the rash you caused with your unshaven face has all gone." Ian lent forward. Suddenly she realised what she had said and so added,

"I don't think I should have said that. I had forgotten that you are not one of my older brothers. I have got three." Ian smiled, although Katie did not see it, as she continued to hold her skirt up so he could get a good look at a beautiful pair of white thighs in the light from the lamp. He thought, '*I suppose having three elder brothers does explain some of her behaviour. I just don't know anything about girls. Do they normally encourage men to look at the top of their thighs? She certainly has very attractive legs. They seem to go up forever and those pink knickers hide very little!*'

The sausages, baked potatoes and salad were very tasty. Then they ate a whole pineapple between them, as Ian said it would be covered in ants by the morning. They had a second beer and then finished up with coffee laced with 'African Cream Liquor'.

Katie felt slightly tipsy. It was very romantic with the wonderful canopy of stars. She was brought down to earth when Ian said,

"You have first shower." She asked,

"Do I shower in my bikini or do you promise not to look. I'm a little shy and the firelight is quite bright." Ian chuckled,

"I promise not to look. It will take all my strength, as you are a very beautiful young lady." She retorted,

"Hopefully you are a very trustworthy gentleman!"

"I am."

Katie did not have a towel so Ian found her one. She actually found it quite comical, as he very purposely sat in the chair pointing away from the shower. Katie found the shower with its hot water marvellous. She suddenly felt less inhibited and relaxed. She was careful to only use half the hot water. She wrapped the towel around her and asked Ian if she could have another towel to wrap around her hair. He laughed,

"I said I had never taken a girl into the NFD. I certainly have never taken a Sikh!" Katie replied,

"Any more cheek from you and I will watch you in the shower. Then I will point at your nether regions and snigger! My brothers always say no man is as well endowed as he would like to be."

"OK, you win. I admit that I'm actually a little shy as well."

Katie was rather amused and reassured by this admission, so while Ian was having his shower she climbed up the ladder and got into her pyjamas. The sleeping bag seemed to be enormous so she wriggled down into it. She thought the mattress was very comfy. She lay to one side and waited to see what would happen.

Ian came up the ladder and got into the tent. He had a brightly coloured sarong type of garment around his waist. He explained to Katie that most people wore them instead of pyjamas as they were cooler. He said they were called '*kikois*'.

Chapter 2

They are both shy at bedtime

Suddenly they were both shy. Ian offered to go and sleep in the Landrover, but Katie said that certainly was not fair and so she started to get out of the sleeping bag. Ian could see she was wearing what in his eyes were extremely sexy pyjamas. They were a little black top with thin straps and French lacy knickers. There eyes met in the torch light. She had unzipped one side. Katie said,

"Come on your biggest, you get in first and I will wriggle in behind you." That's what they did. The sleeping bag was not as big, as it had seemed to Katie, when she was on her own. Ian moved as near to his side as he could, but she could not zip up the sleeping bag behind her. So she had to wriggle around. There was certainly not enough room for them to sleep back to back. So she had to wriggle around again.

Ian naturally was getting excited. He was relieved that at least she was behind him. It was a lovely feeling with her cuddled up to him. She seemed totally unaware of the effect she was having on him. Because she was nervous, she became talkative and moved her arms about. She started to ask him questions about what they were going to do in the morning. She wriggled some more to get comfortable. She slipped her upper arm under his and brought her hand across his chest. Absentmindedly she played with the hairs on his chest. Ian gave a deep sigh,

"Katie, you are so sexy, I will never get to sleep."

"I'm so sorry. I didn't think. Let's both roll over and you cuddle my back."

That's what they then did and of course then she could feel his excitement. However somehow she was not afraid. She pulled his arm over her breast and felt a lovely feeling of being protected. She wriggled one more time and then she went to sleep.

Ian was so aware of her warm body so close to him that he did not calm down very quickly, but eventually he slept.

In the morning at first light they woke. Katie pushed him on to his back and moved on top of him. There was nothing else he could do with his arms so he wrapped them around her. She whispered,

"Thank you for being so kind. I felt so safe last night. Let's just have five more minutes before we have to face the day?"

Because Katie stayed in her pyjamas while she was helping, Ian was hopeless packing up the camp. Every time she did anything which required bending over, he had enormous difficulty in continuing doing what he had been doing. Eventually the tent was collapsed and most of the stuff was in the Landrover. They sat and had bowls of cornflakes at the table. Only then did Katie realise how little of her body was covered. It certainly was cooler than her uniform. She asked,

"Would I upset anyone if I just wore a top and my bikini bottoms?"

"I don't think so. It certainly won't worry me." She got up and lent over into the back of the Landrover into her case and got out a top and her bikini bottoms. Ian thought he had never seen such a sexy sight. She turned and saw him looking,

"Can you just turn around while I change?"

Ian did as he was asked. She ruffled his hair when she had finished,

"Thanks, I knew you were a real Gentleman!"

They finished packing up and got into the Landrover and set off. They got to the first vaccination team in forty minutes. Katie was delighted, as no one seemed to worry about her. They all seemed to be pleased to see in Ian. One of the big vaccine boxes was got out of the Landrover. Various small note-books were checked. Syringes and needles were inspected. Katie found a job for herself, writing down the items which were required by the team. Ian thanked her, as it made his job quicker. It was getting much hotter as the sun got overhead. Katie was glad she was wearing so little, but even so she felt trickles of sweat running down her chest. Before they set off, Ian removed the top half of the doors of the Landrover. He apologised that there would be more dust, but he said he thought she would enjoy the extra air movement. They set off and instantly Katie felt cooler. Ian couldn't help laughing at her, as when they were on a straight, flat, stretch of road without any corrugations, she put her leg out of the vehicle. She laughed with him saying it was much better having a cooling breeze between her thighs than his hot breath like yesterday.

It was in the middle of the afternoon, when they came to a wide river, called the Ewaso Ng'iro which according to Ian meant black water in Masai. It didn't look black now but very muddy. Ian said there must have been heavy rain up in the 'Mathews Hills', where the river had its source. He was reluctant to turn back, as it would add a lot of miles to their journey. He said he would wade through the river to see how deep the water was in the ford. Without thinking about Katie, he took off his shorts and shirt. Katie was surprised, not only that he was not wearing any underpants, but also that he was now naked except for his 'tackies'. Then to her alarm he set off into, what Katie thought looked like, a raging torrent. She took two quick steps into the water and grabbed his arm,

"Stop Ian, you will get washed away." He turned and faced her,

"No, I'll be fine."

"No you won't. At least tie a rope around your waist, so I can hold you." As she said this, her eyes travelled down his body. He saw her glance. He had nothing to cover himself with and stammered,

"I'm so sorry, I forgot I was naked." Katie replied,

"I don't mind that, it's just I don't want to loose you. Please tie a rope round your middle."

So Ian managed to find a rope in the Landrover which he tied with a bowline around his waist. He then attached it to the hook at the end of the cable on the winch on the front of the vehicle. He showed Katie how to work the winch which worked off the battery and so did not require the engine of the Landrover to be switched on. He gave Katie a thick pair of canvass gloves reinforced with leather, so that she would not hurt her hands, as she handled the cable.

He set off again to ford the river. He went really well at first, when the water was just to the middle of his thighs. He started to struggle, when he got to the middle of the river and the water was up to his waist. Then he stumbled, he fell forward and went under. All the time Katie had, not only been paying out the cable, but also keeping it tight. She pressed the switch and the winch started. Initially she still could not see him, as he was pulled down the river by the current, but then the winch took up the slack and to Katie's relief she saw his head come out of the water. He came towards her quite quickly. Katie had the sense to switch off the motor when he was in the shallow water so that he was not dragged up the bank. She ran into the water to help him up. He was not even choking, when she hugged him saying,

"I thought you were going to drown. Thank goodness you are OK."

As she released him she looked down. Her top was soaked and as she wasn't wearing a bra, her breasts were very well outlined. Ian said,

"I think by stopping me blundering into the river, you saved my life with your clever idea. Thank you. I like the wet look." Impulsively she hugged him to her again and said,

"I'll give you, I like the wet look! You are a naughty, cheeky, boy. I am going to make you promise you will be more careful. I am not letting you go across the river without being roped to the winch until the water level is below the tip of your Willy! Now get some shorts on! I think we should make camp back there under those trees. The water is running so fast, I don't think there will be any mosquitos."

Ian tried to muster some dignity, as he walked to the door of the Landrover and retrieved his shorts. He came round the back of the Landrover as Katie was bending over her bag on the ground to find a dry top. He gave her bottom a gentle smack, saying,

"I think Miss. KK, you might have some life saving ideas, but you need taking down a peg or two. Who is charge of this safari?"

Katie turned and gave him a big smile,

"You are of course Mr. IR. As soon as I have a dry top on, I will be your obedient servant."

They locked eyes, as Katie went to take her wet top off. Ian knew she had nothing underneath it. She had called his bluff and he was scared to death. He was the first to look away.

So they made camp in a lovely glade near to the river. After they had made the usual preparations for the camp they were hot and sweaty. They went for a swim in a small pool formed by rocks on the side of the river. This time Ian put on his swimming costume and

Katie put on bikini top as well as the bottom. They laughed together saying they could be at a seaside resort. There was plenty of sand and lots of sun, but the water quality left a lot to be desired.

Katie marvelled at herself, '*Why was she so much more confident? Why did she feel he was so trust worthy? She supposed it had been a gradual feeling culminating in being so close to him during the night. He could have so easily taken advantage of her. Now she realised that actually he was more naïve than her. He knew so little about how to treat girls. The way he was so natural with her was very appealing. Because she had elder brothers made it easier for her, but she knew there was more to it than that. In a strange way she wanted to mother and care for him.*'

She had these thoughts as she was lying on her back on the sand beside the rock pool. She knew he was watching her. '*She did not mind. In fact she was pleased. She could not really understand herself. She would have hated it if the Senior Captain had been watching her beside the swimming pool at the 'Panafric'. Yet he was much smoother and very much more eligible to entertain her and look after her than Ian.*'

Over supper they talked about all manner of different things; His job, the game animals, the tribes in the area and the terrain. They were much more relaxed when they went to bed. Katie wriggled into the sleeping bag first and Ian came in behind her and zipped it up. Katie was sleepy and she just drew his upper arm around her and went to sleep. Although Ian thought it took along time for him to drop off, in reality it was quite quick.

In the early hours of the morning, Katie woke and needed a wee. She tried not to wake him but failed,

"Sorry I did not want to wake you, but now you are awake do you mind guarding me as I have a wee?"

"Of course I don't. I need one as well. The moon is up. We don't need a torch to climb down; it would only spoil our night vision. However you will need your shoes because of the thorns."

He climbed down first and went only a few yards out of the camp. She could see him standing, weeing in the moonlight. She crept up behind him and just as he was dropping down his kikoi, she put her hands on his bare flanks and tickled him. He grabbed her hands and drew her close behind him,

“Now you certainly deserve a good spanking. I got out of my warm bed to help you.”

“Admit it you needed a wee too. Keep looking that way.”

She quickly squatted down, had a wee, jumped up, pulled up her pyjama bottoms and started up the ladder. He was a gentleman and slowly followed her. As she was getting into the sleeping bag she asked,

“Would you really spank me?”

“Of course I wouldn’t.”

“I have read that some girls enjoy it, but I don't think I would.” Then she added as he was getting in behind her, “Why did you give me a very gentle smack yesterday evening?” He answered,

“I'm not really sure. I certainly had no wish to hurt you. I think it was that your pretty bottom was so inviting that I just wanted to touch it, but somehow I hadn't the courage to fondle it.”

“I can feel you now hard behind me. Obviously you can't stop that reaction.”

“No, I'm sorry I can't. Does it worry you? There just is not room for us to sleep back to back.”

“No, it does not worry me. I'm just interested that it is so instantaneous. You only just have to touch me and you are hard. I have read some men don’t get hard except with a lot of encouragement.”

“I suppose we are all different. If I am honest with you, I only have to think about you and I get aroused!” She giggled,

“Should I be frightened? If I am honest with you, I'm pleased. Now I'm being very naughty. I should not have told you that.”

Ian did not answer, but brought his upper arm around her and pulled her gently towards him. She held his hand and moved it over one breast. He loved the feeling through the thin silk. She whispered,

“Wow, he is so hard now, does it hurt. My nipples hurt a little.” Ian took his hand away.

“Please don't stop. It does not really hurt too much. In fact I really like it. I have a strange feeling down below.” She gave a gentle sigh,

“It is a lovely way to go to sleep again. Sleep well.”

They both slept and awoke in the same position. Katie had a very warm feeling of being cared for and did not want the spell to be broken. Then she remembered the river and although there was very little room she rolled to face him,

"Remember your promise yesterday about crossing the river?"

"I don't remember a promise. I just remember instead of a very soft loving Katie, a very bossy Miss. KK talking about the depth of the river relative to a very important part of me."

Katie giggled,

"I think that very important part of you would be well out of the water now." She continued to push up against him,

"Please promise you will be careful, please."

"I will be careful."

They both loved the feeling of closeness and neither of them wanted to move away. She gave him a very gentle kiss on the lips,

"Come on, you have got work to do."

They got up and while Ian went down and revived the fire to make the tea, Katie took off her pyjamas and put on her bikini in the tent. She straightened out everything inside and packed their two bags. Once she had climbed down the ladder and put them in the Landover she collapsed the tent. She was about to secure it, as it had been on the previous day, when she thought about the river. She called to Ian,

"I don't want to be bossy Miss. KK, but should we put all the stuff that we don't want to get wet on the top of the tent on the roof rack?"

"Good idea, tea and breakfast are ready."

After breakfast they both walked down to the river. Ian had made a mark on a tree with his panga on the previous day. The river was still deep, but it had dropped nearly two feet.

When they were ready, Ian lifted the bonnet and took off the fan belt from the engine, as he said that would lessen the danger of the plugs, coil and distributor being splashed. He found some special wax spray which he sprayed over all the electrics.

They returned and got into the Landrover. Katie stayed behind to do a check of the campsite to make sure that they had not left anything and then hopped up into the vehicle. They set off, Ian knew that without the fan belt he must get going fairly quickly or the engine would get too hot. As they came down the slope of the bank in four wheel drive and low range, Katie turned to him,

"Good luck."

They churned through the river relatively slowly, but with Ian keeping the revs up and letting the front of the Landrover make a bow wave, they made it across and up the other bank. As he was leaning over putting the fan belt back on, Katie impulsively put arms around him from behind and kissed the back of his neck. The lovely feel of her virtually naked body, did not help his concentration!

When he had finished and they had undone the ropes, Katie climbed on the roof rack and handed the kit down to him. She said,

"I'm sorry I made us all that extra work."

"No it was a very sensible idea. Anyhow I am now getting a lovely view with you leaning down!" Katie's whole body seemed to blush.

"I am cross with myself. Why am I so embarrassed? Anyway, thanks for the compliment."

They arrived at the next vaccination team only just in time, as they had nearly run out of vaccine. Ian explained to them about the problems of the river at Barsalinga. Once again, Katie made herself useful by noting down all their stores requirements.

They soon set off and started to climb into the Mathews range. Ian told her it would be cold camping tonight. He said he had some extra blankets. He smiled at her, when he said that he did think it would not be so cold with two of them in the sleeping bag. She said

"So I do have my uses then!"

"You are the prettiest hot water bottle I have had!" Katie flicked her pony tail,

"I thought you said I was the first girl you had taken into the NFD?"

"Usually I heat up a big rock. It does not give me so much cheek!"

"So I'm compared to a big rock, am I? I hope you enjoyed spanking the big rock! I suppose you did not have to, as it did not give you any cheek. Was it good fun cuddling it?"

"At least it did not wake me up in the middle of the night for a wee." Katie laughed,

"From what you have said, it is going to be bloody cold having a wee tonight."

"You're right. I bet you won't be brave enough to have a bath or swim in the little river."

Luckily they got to their camping spot early, so they both had a quick dip in the water, which was hardily more that a small fast running stream. It was freezing. When they got out Ian explained, as he was hugging her that they were at six thousand feet.

Chapter 3

Nearly a disaster on the third night

The sun went down and it became really misty. Ian managed to find some dry wood so they made a good fire. Katie was soon getting more clothes on. She put on her stockings and suspender belt much to Ian's enjoyment. They had a good supper. They ate it quickly and were soon in the tent. They brought their coffees and the 'African Cream' up with them. By the time they were actually getting into bed. Katie felt a little tipsy and very sexy. She kept her blouse and sweater on, but took off her trousers. She got into the sleeping bag first. Ian was sorting out the two extra blankets, so that they were over the top of the sleeping bag. He then took off all is clothes and wrapped his kikoi around his waist. Once he was in the sleeping bag he managed to zip it up. Katie said,

"Won't you be cold? I have got most of my clothes on." Ian replied,

"I think you will be too hot. I am too hot already. Just thinking about your suspender belt has pushed up my temperature by ten degrees."

Katie wriggled her bottom, very provocatively. She knew his kikoi had ridden up and she felt his Willy on her thighs above her stocking tops. She realised that she had got herself into a bit of a muddle. Her knickers were over the top of her suspenders. Ideally she should take her knickers off, unclipped her stockings, take them off, take off her suspender belt and then put her knickers back on. Whatever, there was going to be a lot of scrabbling about. Why ever had she drunk so much? Bloody hell she felt sexy. She decided to be honest, well at least partially so.

"Ian, I am a bit pissed and have got myself into a bit fix with my underwear. Like you I am getting seriously hot. Will you be a real gentleman and help me sort myself out, so we can go to sleep at the right temperature?"

“Of course, what do you want me to do?”

“I will unclip my stockings. Will you carefully take them off with your longer arms, preferably without laddering them?”

“OK.” Katie very carefully unclipped her left stocking. She was dying to touch his Willy with her hand to see what it felt like. Breathlessly she said,

“Now can you take my left stocking off?” She felt his hands on her right thigh. She whispered,

“That’s the wrong leg, you numpty!” Katie felt a very nice sensation in her tummy as he fiddled around her upper thighs and gently rolled down her stocking. She then giggled,

“I don't know why I am whispering. I doubt if there is another human being for fifty miles. Now you have your hands down there, I think it would be easier if you unclipped the other stocking.” She giggled again, as she felt his hand.

“Thank goodness I have only got two legs. You won't make a mistake this time! What are you doing? You have no need to check my thighs. The rash your chin caused has completely gone.”

She thought, ‘*I'm being very naughty, but this is great fun.*’

The other stocking came off. Katie knew how excited Ian was getting, but somehow she just could not stop. He was behind her in the sleeping bag, so it would be practically more sensible for him to take her knickers off. She thought, ‘*really Katie is this wise to ask a guy to take your knickers off? He is so lovely and kind, but it will be testing him to his limit.*’ She threw caution to the wind and said in a very matter of fact voice,

“Can you just slip my knickers off?” She heard his sharp intake of breath and then felt him slowly push down her knickers, first over her hips, then over her bottom. It was just when her knickers were over the top of her thighs that she felt his Willy spring up between them. She knew he could not help it. In a strange way she could not stop herself from opening her legs a little. Then she felt it touch her. She was already moist and somehow she felt the tip just enter her. Neither of them could stop. She pushed her bottom towards him. He pulled her thighs towards him. She felt more of him inside her. Then Ian cried,

“No Katie, my darling girl, we mustn't go any further!” He pulled her knickers back up. They both were breathing really hard. He pulled down the zip of the sleeping bag and rolled out on to his back. She rolled on top of him crying,

"You are right what was I thinking? You are such a kind man, Ian. You deserve a better girl than me."

"Nonsense, you are so lovely. You deserve a better man than me. I'm a rough old vet. You are so beautiful you should be a top model." She kissed him passionately. He put his hands on her bottom as they broke apart, saying,

"We must only kiss like that when your beautiful little bottom is safe in some knickers!" She replied,

"I just can't believe I told you to take them off. I was so naughty. I can easily take my suspender belt off without taking my knickers off." She then unhooked the belt and pulled it away from her body. They ended up zipped back in the sleeping bag with Ian cuddling her back, with her in a blouse and her knickers. That's how they were when they woke in the morning. She wriggled round and kissed him. She then said,

"Wow, what a night. I'm not sure if I have lost my virginity or not, but thank you for being so lovely. I just know if we had not stopped, I would have got pregnant, which would have been disastrous. I know I had drunk too much, but I just wanted you so much. Will you forgive me for being so wanton?" He kissed her neck and murmured,

"You do talk a lot of rubbish. I was just as much to blame."

From then on the safari flew by. Ian worked hard and Katie loved helping him. They found some great camping places. They both became more uninhibited. Katie was appalled and excited by her lack of shyness, when they were totally on their own out in the NFD. She was quite happy being in the nude, but she always wore either her pyjama bottoms or her knickers in the sleeping bag. They had a particularly memorable night in the forest on Marsabit Mountain. They camped by a crater lake. Elephant cows and calves came down to drink in the dusk. It got really cold and they needed the extra blankets. When they got into the sleeping bag, Ian pulled the blankets over them and whispered,

"I think you will be too hot in those knickers!"

"Nice try, but you will have to dream on." Then she giggled,

“You know I want you to take them off. I dream of that feeling as you pulled them over my hips. It's lucky I have a big bottom or you might have got them down quicker and I would be pregnant by now.”

“You haven't got a big bottom!”

“Even better try.” Then she kissed his neck and he hugged her to him.

After they had delivered the vaccine to the veterinary office in Marsabit, Ian decided to take a short cut through the forest to check up on a vaccination team down on the slopes of the mountain towards the Chalbis Desert. Just on the edge of the forest they were waved down by a Rendile tribesman. His friend was lying on the ground. For one second, Ian thought it was a trick to get a lift. Katie had seen the bleeding and was getting out. Ian shouted,

“Katie, you must be careful it may be a trick.”

Katie just disregarded him and ran to the man on the ground. She had never seen so much blood. It was coming out of a large hole in his chest. She whipped off her top and rolled it into a pad. She pushed that into the hole in his chest. Ian had now seen the problem. He managed to find a roll of cling film in the Landrover. Then they wrapped cling film tightly around the man’s chest, keeping the pad in place. Ian quickly made a flat place in the back of the Landrover. Katie got in first to hold the injured man, after Ian and his friend had lifted him in. They immediately set off to Marsabit Hospital. Ian talked to the man beside him and translated for Katie. It appeared that the pair had come out of the forest and spooked a rhino. It had charged and then hit the man in the chest with its horn before turning round and disappearing into the trees.

At the district hospital was a qualified English surgeon who was gaining experience in this remote place and who also was teaching two Kenyan medics who hoped to become surgeons. So the injured man was to receive amazingly good treatment in what really was hardly more than a bush hospital. Staying with the surgeon was a college friend who was a freelance journalist and photographer. When he saw Katie wearing only her bikini bottoms, covered in blood nursing the tribesman, he snapped off a real of film. He knew the photos were pure gold. He was due to fly with two missionaries later that morning to Nairobi and then on the night flight to London. He wrote his article on the plane.

Katie and Ian were both delighted, as because the work and the travelling had gone so well, they got back a day ahead of schedule, so not only could Katie come and see his home, but also they could have a lie in the following morning.

Ian had a cook called Nelson. He welcomed Katie with a smile and a handshake. Ian whispered when they were alone,

"He obviously likes the look of you, he very rarely smiles."

Katie was delighted with Ian's bathroom which had the most enormous bath. Ian said he rarely used it as he normally had a shower. Katie asked if they could have a bath together. Before he could answer she added that she was going to have a decent wash ALL OVER! She had a fit of the giggles at the worried look on his face. Then she became very serious and said,

"Don't worry we will be very careful."

They couldn't wait to get into a proper bed. As Katie's pyjamas were dirty, she had put them in Ian's laundry basket, as he said that Nelson would do her washing. They both knew that her leaving clothes at his house were symbolic of a long-term relationship.

Ian got into bed first. Katie came in from the bathroom in the nude laughing,

"I'm not much of a girl friend. I should come into your bedroom and strip for you. Instead I have come in naked and I am going to put some knickers on. At least they are clean. This is a real treat to sleep in a proper bed. I'm pleased it is only a single one. We will have to cuddle up nice and close or one of us will fall out!

The knickers did stay on and we're still on in the morning. However Ian, much to Katie's delight, did manage to put his hand down the front of them!

They both were sad on the drive out to the airport as they had no idea how Katie was going to get out again to Nairobi. She gave him a big kiss in the Landrover. After he had got her case out of the back she said,

"I'm like a bad penny, I'll be back." She blew him a kiss and went into Departures. Now she thought I have got to face the pilot and the rest of the crew.

She was slightly later than them. They had come through immigration and we're all having a coffee. The cabin crew were on one table and the three from the flight deck on another.

Their safari had been OK and in fact they had seen lots of game, but the atmosphere had never really become friendly. The girls actually had felt sorry that they had been bitchy to Katie and now they guessed that she had been lonely on her own in Nairobi and had to face them for the flight home. The friendliest called Nicola saw Katie and waved. She was pleased that Katie walked over to them and did not seem to be put out by how nasty they had been to her. Nicola bought her a coffee and Katie asked Yvonne the head air hostess whether they had seen lots of game. Yvonne could see Katie was very brown and replied,

"Yes, we did see a large amount, but I think I can speak for all of us. We found it very tiring and we all would have welcomed a few days relaxing in the sun. So I don't think you missed much. You certainly have got a tan."

They all chatted then about the game they had seen and the lodges they had visited. Katie politely listened.

The Chief Pilot had managed to buy a 'Sunday Times'. He was scanning through the colour supplement looking at photos of a girl covered in blood nursing an African who apparently had been gored by a rhino. He could not believe his eyes, when he saw the centre fold. It was a full frontal of Katie just in her bikini bottoms holding the injured man while a European and another African lifted him out of the back of a Landrover. The caption was, 'Eighteen year old Katie Kent nurses a severely injured Rendile Tribesman. She had used her top to stem the haemorrhage from his chest. Then she had wrapped the man in cling film. She held the man close to her, while her friend Ian Richardson brought him into a remote hospital in Kenya's NFD.'

He walked over to the air hostess's and slapped the supplement on the table, saying to Katie,

"You shouldn't be an air hostess. You should be a bloody model for 'Playboy'."

Katie did not have a clue what he was talking about, but had certainly had enough of him and no longer cared that he could get her taken off 'long-haul'. She stood up and retorted,

"You have got a bloody nerve. I had my pyjamas on when you barged into my room. You are dam lucky that I haven't reported you to the personnel department. I wish I had aimed for your head rather than your shoulder, when I hit you with that bedside light. Bugger off and go and do your preflight checks!"

She turned to Nicola and said,

"I wish you had bought me a brandy. I think I need one."

The Chief pilot turned on his heel and left. The other girls crowded around the magazine. Yvonne showed it to Katie.

"Did he really barge into your room?" Katie answered,

"I was a fool I thought it was one of you. I suppose he will get me the sack now, not just taken off 'long-haul'." Yvonne replied aggressively,

"Not if I can do anything about it. What do you say girls? Do you want Katie to join us permanently?" There was general agreement. They all wanted to know what Katie had been up to.

Chapter 4

A 24 Hour Emergency Stop Over

Katie stayed with Yvonne's crew. The flight crew were moved and two different pilots and another navigator joined them. Three weeks later, Katie and her crew were delayed in Johannesburg because of an electrical fault on their VC10. When they got to Nairobi they had to be stood down, as they would have run out of hours, if they had continued to Heathrow. They were taken in two shuttle buses to the 'Panafric Hotel'. When they were all checking in, Katie asked the hotel to book a taxi to Kabete. Nicola asked,

"Are you going to be antisocial as normal, Katie?" Katie just hoped Ian would be at home and replied,

"My friend might be at home." She walked out pulling her airline case to the waiting taxi. She got in the front with the driver saying,

"Can I sit with you, so you can teach me some Swahili?" He smiled,

"*Ndio Memsahib. Habari ake?* (Yes Madam. How are you?)"

"*Mzuri sana. Habari?* (I am very well. How are you?)" Then she asked him the Swahili names for everything they saw. The driver thought she was hilarious.

When she arrived at Ian's house, she was disappointed as his Landrover was not in the drive. Her spirits lifted when Nelson came out to welcome her. He carried her case in while she paid the taxi. She had had the sense to keep some Kenyan Shillings from her previous visit. Katie smiled, as Nelson knew the form and put her case in Ian's room. He told her that Ian had gone to play rugby at 'Nondescripts'. She said to Nelson that she had been a fool and had let the taxi go off. Nelson replied that she did not have to worry, as he had heard the Bwana talking to Mr Cramp who lived next door. Mr Cramp was going into 'Westlands' in half an hour. Nelson said he would go and see Mr. Cramp and, that he was sure Mr. Cramp would help her get to 'Nondescripts'. Katie thanked him. She thought she would have a quick shower and get out of her airline uniform and put on a pretty dress. As always she was dying to take off her stockings. She came out of the bathroom into the hall, wrapped in a fairly revealing towel to be met by a strange, middle aged, man, whose face lit up,

"Hello, I'm Basil Cramp. Nelson tells me that you would like a lift to 'Westlands'." He held out his hand. Katie held out hers and nearly lost her towel. Basil's smile grew wider. Katie said,

"I'm sorry to hold you up; I will quickly get some clothes on."

"Yes, that might be a good idea!" Katie had wanted to make herself as pretty as possible, but now she had to leave her hair wet and quickly get dressed. All her dresses were fashionable with a full skirt to mid-calf. She ran out into the drive to find Basil sitting on an enormous motorbike. He was still grinning,

"I hope you don't mind. I'm a bit of an enthusiast." Katie thought, '*Well my hair will dry and then it will be in a hell of a mess. I have no make-up on and my dress is going to blow up and the whole of Nairobi is going to see my sexy French knickers!*'

Basil dropped her at 'Parklands' and pointed out the rugby pitch and 'Nondescripts' clubhouse. She felt very alone as she walked across. She was just thankful that everyone was looking in the other direction, watching the game, until the ball was kicked into touch well over the heads of all the spectators. Katie had not had three elder brothers who had been mad keen on rugby for nothing. She caught the ball by making a basket of her arms, as they had taught her. She took a couple of steps forward and showing quite a large amount of leg, punted the ball back in the direction from where it had come. A cheer went up from the spectators who had all turned to watch her. She felt herself blush, as she walked on towards them. Two eight year old boys who had been running to retrieve the ball came up to her. One said in admiration,

"Wow that was a good kick." The other said,

"Whose girl friend are you?" Katie laughed,

"I looked a mess before I caught that ball. Look at me now. I expect I'm not anyone's girl friend as messy as this?" The mud from the ball was all down the front of her dress. She added,

"Come on you two. Make me less embarrassed by holding my hands."

So Katie arrived and joined the spectators. The boy's mother who was called Jean said,

"You should be highly honoured, I can never get Derek and Robert to hold my hands and I'm their mother!"

"I am honoured. Can you tell me the form? Who is playing who? I have just been driven here on a motor bike and I'm a bit blown away." Jean answered,

"'Nondescripts' in white are playing against 'Harlequins'." Katie asked,

"Wow, have they come from England?" Jean laughed,

"No there is a local club with the same name. My husband plays for 'Nondescripts'. They are losing. He won't be very pleased." Katie enquired in the most casual voice she could manage,

"Do you know Ian Richardson? I arrived at his house. He wasn't expecting me and his cook said he was playing." Jean showed some surprise.

"Are you his girl friend? He's certainly kept very quiet about you." Katie was slightly embarrassed.

"Well I'm not sure girl friend quite describes me. He has taken me on a very rough safari once." Jean smiled,

"I knew I had seen your face before. You were the stunning girl who featured with him in the Sunday Times Colour Supplement." An older man who was standing near them, chipped in,

"I don't remember your face but you've got great tits!" Jean said in a whisper,

"Watch out for Reggie. His hand tends to wander on to your bottom." Katie whispered back,

"Thanks for the warning."

'Nondescripts' then scored. There was a roar from the home crowd. Derek told Katie that if Nondescripts converted the try then they needed another try and a conversion to win. Katie started to cheer for 'Nondescripts'. Robert told her rather despondently that they would never do it, as they were in injury time.

It certainly was an exciting match as 'Nondescripts' were really driving forward in the middle of the pitch. There were lots of short passes between the forwards. Katie joined the 'Nondescripts' supporters cheering like mad and jumping up and down. They were in the Harlequins twenty five. Somehow Ian managed to break away with the ball. At least Katie thought it was Ian, but he was so muddy she could not be certain. He was five yards out and he dived, scoring a try under the posts. The crowd went wild. Mercifully the 'Nondescript's' full back made no mistake with the conversion.

Derek and Robert grabbed her hands and pulled her on to the pitch. She did not need much more encouragement. She ran to Ian and wrapped her arms around his muddy body.

"Well done, you are a real star."

"Katie, however did you get here?" Then he kissed her.

When they broke apart he said,

"My Darling girl, I've made a real mess of your dress." Katie just laughed. She had only once been called 'My Darling girl' before.

Jean lent forward and whispered to her husband.

"Her name is Katie and she tried to act very casual, but this is obviously something big. She seems a lovely girl and certainly does not mind getting dirty. I think she will suit Ian rather well."

The party after the rugby game was a riot. The players all had sausages and mashed potatoes, so they at least had something to line their stomachs with. Katie had way too many G & Ts. Her excuse to Ian in the Landrover on the way home was that she needed something to hide her embarrassment for her very muddy dress. She cuddled up to him by sitting in the middle seat,

"I so wanted to look pretty for you. Now you will have to make do with my new pyjamas. You liked the last pair. These are white, lacy and even more revealing." Ian groaned,

"Will the bottoms keep me out?" Katie answered just a little bit too casually. Ian, if he had been sober, would have picked up on it.

"Oh well we will just have to see."

Ian was the first into bed. He no longer bothered with a 'kikoi'. They only got rucked up or came undone. He had forgotten how Katie had managed to get a wonderful all over tan just by wandering about in the nude, when they were in camp out in the wilds.

She came in having cleaned her teeth. The white pyjamas were certainly lacy. The top had tiny straps and was very low cut. It ended a couple of inches above the tiniest pair of bottoms which he could imagine. He gasped,

"Katie you look amazing. I want to kiss every part of you." With a cheeky smile she replied,

"That's rather what I had in mind when I bought them!"

She got in beside him, wriggled her body, so that she was touching him in as many places as she possibly could and then she kissed him. She teased him with her tongue. She rubbed herself against him. She loved the feel of his hands through the silk of her top. Soon he had taken it off and seemed to be kissing her every where. She was mewing with pleasure as she whispered,

"Can you take my bottoms off? He slid his hands down her waist and then stopped,

"Oh Katie, this is so dangerous!" Rather breathlessly she replied,

"I just hoped I could get out here and so I have been very naughty. I am on the pill. I want to feel you properly inside of me. I am so ready for you."

She lifted her bottom so he could gently take off her bottoms. Then he slid down and his mouth came down on her and his tongue started to do the most delightful things. She just clutched his head and panted,

"That is so good. You must stop. No don't stop. Oh yes, Oh yes." Her pelvis was trusting up to him. Her legs were wide open with her feet flat on the bed. She gave one more cry,

"Yes, take me now."

She hardily felt him enter her. She was too weak to thrust now and just let him rhythmically pull her bottom to him. Then she held him as he shuddered to a climax. He was her man and she was his woman. Neither of them knew how long they lay there, but eventually they kissed and then they slept.

Sometime in the night they moved into their normal position with him cuddling her back and his hands cupping her breasts. With delight she felt him hard again. She reached behind her and guided him. Soon there was no stopping him. He seemed to be rubbing in just the right spot and they both climaxed together, sighing. They slept until morning.

Ian had given Nelson the day off so Ian made the tea and brought it to the bedroom. He was greeted by Katie stretching her arms to him, saying,

"I have never had another lover, but I'm sure you are all a girl could wish for. I think I'm meant to feel sore, but if you let me have a wee, then I want you again.

When he was on top of her, she said,
"On second thoughts, may be a cup of tea would be better!"
They virtually spent the whole day in bed. Katie had to be all dressed in her uniform by 7.30pm. They were nearly at the airport by 7.15. Katie got him to stop in a lay-by and give her a proper kiss. Then she put on her lipstick and as they arrived at Departures she jumped out saying,
"See you as soon as I possibly can. That was a wonderful cup of tea this morning!" Then she was off walking and pulling her case across the floor to join the others. One air hostess said,
"You look as if you have won the lottery." Katie replied,
"You could put it that way!"

Katie and the crew had a stop over at Cape Town, where she spent two days topping up her tan. However when she heard that they are scheduled to have a short time at Nairobi on the way back to the UK she sent Ian a telegram.
Arriving 7.30pm at Embakasi. Not allowed out of the airport but would love a cup of tea! xxxxx
In her haste to get out of the arrivals building, Katie walked straight by Ian so he came up behind her and made her jump,
"Would Madam like to step this way for her cup of tea?" She gave him a big kiss and said breathlessly,
"It is a real bugger; I have only got twenty minutes." Ian replied,
"Come on don't let's waste a minute."
He led her to his Landrover which was parked around the corner. He opened the rear door, to reveal that he had made up a single bed in the back. He has also rigged up curtains on the windows. The bed was rather high up, as it had to rest on the bench back seats running down either side. Katie grumbled,
"How am I going to get up there in this tight skirt?"
"That's easy." Before she could object, he pulled up her skirt, put an arm between her legs and hoisted her face down on to the mattress. Then he jumped on top of her pulling the door closed behind him. He started kissing the back of her neck and doing wicked things with his hand between her legs. Katie struggled,
"Ian, you must stop, some one might look in the windows. Oh Ian that is so lovely. Ian you must stop my knickers are too tight. Bloody

hell I didn't mean you to rip them." She groaned as he mounted her from behind. She stopped worrying about her skirt which is around her waist and pushed up and back in time with him. He had one hand around her waist rubbing her. She bit into the pillow, and grabbed the blanket with both hands. Katie just lay under him panting, as she felt him slipping out of her. Then she whispered,

"Bloody hell, that was quick, I think that gives you ten minutes to tell me your news, while I sort myself out. By the way, you owe me a very expensive pair of knickers. I bought them specially, as I thought I my might get a chance to show you some thigh!"

Chapter 5

A trip on a cattle boat

Katie and her crew got a stop over for three nights in Mombasa. The rest of the crew are pleased as they get booked into the big 'Oceanic Hotel' on Mombasa Island. They can relax in the sun all day by the big pool. Katie has other plans. Ian is taking her on what he describes as a rough tropical cruise with a night on a romantic island called Lamu where he promises the accommodation will definitely be sub-standard.

Katie gets in one of the mini-buses with the rest and they head out of the airport to Mombasa Island. Ian has given her instructions, so she asks the driver to drop her on the causeway on to Mombasa Island at the entrance to the Kenya Meat Commission (KMC). They come down the dual carriageway and they start to smell a revolting smell. The other girls complain to the driver who explains that the smell comes from many places; the public tip, the town dairies, the veterinary office and KMC. Katie's heart sinks, but she trusts Ian so as they swing into the entrance of KMC she gets out of the mini-bus, shouting goodbye to the other girls who urge the driver to get going away from the smell.

Katie is made of stern stuff, she starts to walk into the abattoir. She is met by what seems like hundreds of Africans, clad in white overalls which are covered in blood, riding bicycles. On the back of each bike is a long thin piece of meat. Then to her relief she sees Ian running towards her. He gives her a hug and she asks,

"Whatever are those pieces of meat on these guy's bicycles?" Ian laughs,

"Yes, they do look rather gruesome. They are oxtails, called a '*mkia*', in Swahili. Each worker gets one as a perk for the job on top of his wages." Katie smiles,

"Well, this air hostess wants a bit of '*mkia*', as a perk for being told to come to this dreadful place! Oh well you do specialise in rough adventures. Has the cruise liner docked yet?"

Ian replies,

"Yes, she is called the 'Bonanza'. Let me carry your flight bag, the loading ramp is a little shitty from her previous passengers for you to pull your case. Katie grimaces, but follows Ian. On her left is the enormous white abattoir but ahead, where Ian is leading is a wooden stockade. Ian opens the gate and before her is a three hundred yard cattle race with wooden sides. The surface is concrete and is covered in cattle dung. Ian looks at her smart shoes and then at her face.

"Would you like a piggy-back?" Very calmly she replied,

"Thank you, kind Sir. That would be very helpful. However you are going to struggle with me and my case, so I think I will have to forget my modesty and you had better give me a fireman's lift!"

Looking straight at him smirking, she lifted up her knee length uniform skirt, showing her stocking tops and parts her legs. Ian puts his right arm between them, she falls on to his back. Ian straightens up and picks up her case with his left hand and sets off down the cattle race. Katie says,

"I'm glad the rest of the crew can't see me now!" He replied,

"Anyhow all they would see is your petit bottom which certainly does not look big in that skirt!"

"You know Ian sometimes you say just the right things. I might find a use for that '*mkia'* of yours after all!"

As she was being carried half upside down, Katie did not see the cattle boat, until Ian gently set her down at the end of the gang plank. She was no overly impressed by the shoddy appearance of the boat, but at least they could walk aboard up the human gangway which was free of cattle dung. At the top Katie was met by an immaculately dressed Arab in a brilliantly white kansu and wearing a red fez who welcomed her on board. Ian had been on earlier to dump his kit. The Arab's name was Shatri. He showed Katie to their cabin which had bunk beds, a separate shower and a lavatory. Shatri said,

"*Memsahib* I have been talking to *Bwana* Richardson and I wondered if you would care to use this cabin as a day cabin, and as it is a little hot at night, use the large bed in the saloon to sleep on, if we carried it above the cattle pens?" Katie replied,

"Shatri, I think that sounds an excellent idea."

Shatri told them that he expected the Captain who had been ashore getting supplies together with the rest of the crew, to be on board soon. Then they would cast off and commence their journey.

As soon as they were alone, much to Ian's delight, Katie stripped off. She knew he was watching her, so she made it as sexy as possible. She teased him, as he broke out in a sweat just from watching her. Katie did not rush to put any clothes on, but sat on the lower bunk.

"Normally I like the smell of cows, but this is a little over powering."

"Sadly it will be much worse on the return journey when we have three hundred on board!"

Katie, always the one to see the best of any situation replied,

"Oh well, I will be more used to it by then. You're a bit slow today. I have been sitting here in the nude for five minutes, what's the delay?"

Ian rather sheepishly started taking his clothes off.

"I thought you would be too hot?" Katie laughed as she climbed on to the top bunk.

"As I'm ready first, I'm choosing to be on top. There are three good cold air blowers up here. Come on! I feel sexy. Let's see that '*mkia*' of yours."

As Ian clambered on to the top bunk, Katie pushed him on to his back and lay on top of him,

"You know I like to straddle you but I'm frightened of hitting my head."

They she started kissing him. Their tongues played with each other. Katie reached down to hold him. Ian said,

"Have I ever told you are wonderful?" Katie chuckled,

"Yes, you have, in fact normally you do when I have a good grip on your '*mkia*'. I love the feel of it when it is all hard. Do you like me holding it?" Ian gasped,

"It is bloody lovely when you rub it on you."

Katie was getting aroused now. Soon she collapsed on top of him. She then totally relaxed, as Ian stroked her hair. She dropped off to sleep. Ian let her sleep; as he knew she must be pretty tired after working on a long flight. Then he slept with her.

They were awoken by the throbbing of the ship's engines. They got down from the top bunk and had a shower. The shower cubicle was tiny, so Katie made Ian just standstill and she washed him. Then he washed her. Katie reckoned as a cleaning exercise it was rubbish, but as a sexy wash it was good fun. They guessed that as The Kenyan Coast was so hot they would be doing a lot of showering. They got dressed and went up on deck. Ian had warned Katie that the Danish Skipper was a kind old man, but sadly was an alcoholic. Katie wondered how safe the journey would be, but Ian assured her that the African crew knew the form.

They came up on deck as the 'Bonanza' slipped its moorings and headed out to sea via Tudor Creek and then under Nyali Bridge.

The Captain came up to them and introduced himself to Katie saying that he was called Olaf. Katie told him about Shatri's idea with the bed. Olaf said he had no objections whatsoever and asked if she wanted the bed moved now, so she could do some sunbathing. Katie knew what he was after, but thought, '*What the hell. It might be safer for all of us if he spends time looking at me rather than having a drink!*'

Ian helped the crew move the bed which was large and solid. The crew had obviously moved it before, as they soon roped it down on the roof of the cattle pens. Katie smiled as she could see she would be on view to Olaf on the bridge. She found Shatri in the galley and asked him if he minded that she did some sunbathing. She said she knew that his wife or girl friend would never do anything like that. She said she would hate to offend him. Shatri smiled, but said he would not be offended. He said he would only be offended if either of his two wives exposed themselves in such a manner. Katie was intrigued and asked whether his two wives spent time together. Shatri was surprised by the question and said,

"Oh yes, they are really good friends."

Katie was amazed. Later as she was stretched out in sun she wondered whether she could ever be friends with any girl that was also a current sexual partner of Ian's. She thought that, when she was on her own with him she would ask him what he thought.

There was only a very light wind coming from the North East and so the motion of the ship when it reached the open sea was very relaxing. Also the gentle breeze with the forward speed of the boat removed the smell of cattle. Katie had a very enjoyable afternoon. She hoped the rest of the air-crew was enjoying their break. While she was sunbathing, Ian was in the saloon having a cold beer, in fact several cold beers with Olaf. Katie's idea of reducing Olaf's consumption had not worked.

Obviously, as they were out at sea there were no mosquitos and so Katie only went down for a shower when it was dark. She then joined the men for supper. She could see Ian was slightly the worst for wear, but the beer did not seem to have had any effect on Olaf. Supper was quite lively. Olaf was smitten by Katie. She ate and drank very little, as she was slightly worried about seasickness although she had never been seasick before. However Olaf assured her that the wind would actually drop and so they would have a dead calm trip. He teased Ian saying he did not need to tie her to the bed in case she fell out. Then he guffawed saying that perhaps she might enjoy being tied to the bed. Katie blushed, but did not say anything.

It felt a little strange to Katie as she cleaned her teeth, wrapped herself in Ian's kikoi, as she had not brought any pyjamas and went up to bed. Ian soon followed her. He just stripped off and got on to the bed. She whispered,

"I feel slightly shy, but this is very exotic. The stars are so bright. Are you a bit pissed?"

"Yes, I am. I know what you mean about being a little exposed up here, but it is lovely and cool compared to the cabin." Katie replied,

"I think I will just go down to the cabin and bring up a sheet."

When she came back up she smiled, as Ian was stark naked lying on his back, fast asleep. She thought, '*So much for our romantic cruise; however I wonder what tomorrow will bring? A bit of a headache for the man I love I think.*' She covered Ian with the sheet and then wriggled in beside him. He was dead to the world, so she just snuggled up to him and went to sleep in the beautiful cool air.

Ian woke in the night and was not quite sure where he was. He didn't wake her, but had a wee and drank a couple of pints of water. He had to get up twice more in the night! The third time he woke, it was about an hour before dawn, Katie woke with him. She teased him whispering,

"Last night you were sensational!"

"Was I? All I can remember was being a bit pissed!"

"I was teasing you. You old fool. You were bloody useless. You just passed out! Are you up to anything now?" He didn't reply but nuzzled her neck which she thought was a good sign. Slowly he became more aroused. Katie made sure he brought her with him and would not let him into her until she was ready and he was frantic. As he collapsed on top of her she gasped,

"Thank you for that, but I bloody well had to wait for it." They slept until the dawn was just coming and then went down to their cabin, her wrapped in his kikoi and him, like a ghost wrapped in a sheet. They soon went and had a good breakfast with Olaf who seemed on top form, none the worse for his drinking the previous night. They joined him on the bridge as he brought the boat in between Lamu Island on the right and the mainland on the left. Both shores were covered by thick mangrove swamps. The tide was half way out so Katie could see the black sticky mud under the trees. They came to an opening on the mainland, where there was a small village called Mkowe. They moored up along side a jetty and a cattle race similar to the race at the KMC. However this time Katie was not in her smart working clothes and so was not worried about a bit of dry cattle dung. She and Ian came ashore with his veterinary kit and their few over night clothes, leaving their other bags on board.

Katie was delighted that all the veterinary staff seemed so pleased to see Ian and this enthusiastic welcome extended to her. They were soon off in a Landrover driven by a driver called 'Karissa', which Katie thought should be a girl's name but this man was big and not at all girlie. She was crammed into the middle seat between him and Ian. She thought they were tightly packed, until she looked into the back of the Landrover. There did not seem to be an inch to spare. She whispered to Ian,

"This is a government vehicle. Am I allowed in it?" Ian responded,

"Don't worry things are very relaxed in the north in the Coast Province."

The road was really a soft sand track. 'Karissa' obviously fancied himself as a bit of a rally driver, so they drifted round the numerous corners through the bush. Katie rather enjoyed the ride and gave Ian's thigh a little stroke. She noticed the bulge and thought, '*I don't think that would have happened last night at bedtime!"*

They arrived after twenty minutes at Burgoni holding ground. Three hundred large, big, white, steers with large humps and big dewlaps were corralled in some wooden pens. A group of thirty were immediately driven into one of two long cattle races. The head of the front steer was gripped by two large men each clad in only a thin cloth skirt which totally failed to cover their manhood. Another man in khaki uniform who Katie gathered was a veterinary scout, pulled out the tongue of the poor beast. Ian examined the tongue carefully. The animal's head was released, but it was still kept in the race. The next animal was examined and so on. While this was going on, more cattle were driven into the neighbouring race. Katie saw they were pushed up tight by men pulling on their tails, with their heads all in the same direction. When all the animals in one race had been examined, they were released and wandered into the bush watched by more scantily clad men.

The process carried on. Another Landrover arrived with a jovial Asian man called Suleiman, who was the District Livestock Office (DLO) for Lamu district. He apologised for not being at Mkowe when they arrived. He said that 'Bonanza' had docked a little earlier than normal and so he had come across in the veterinary boat from Lamu Island as quickly as he could. The cattle examinations continued, but the operation speeded up as Suleiman also examined the tongues. Ian explained to Katie that they were looking for lesions of Foot and Mouth Disease (FMD) as it would be disastrous if an animal arrived for slaughter at KMC suffering from FMD. It was a new idea of Ian's to make sure this disaster did not happen.

When all three hundred had been examined, Suleiman produced a thermos of hot coffee and some mugs. Ian explained to Katie that hot drinks did not bring you out in a sweat like cold drinks. She explained to him that horses sweat, men perspire and girls just got hot. He asked,

"So I am just imagining your shirt wet through, sticking to your body?"

"Yes that's right; I'm just a little hot!" Suleiman who spoke English laughed and produced a paper bag of Samosas which he offered to Katie and Ian. It was Katie's time to laugh, as she bit into one, before saying,

"Now I am seriously hot, but of course I'm not sweating!"

It seemed as if the day's work was over, so they all got into the two Landrovers and headed back to Mkowe. They got on board the veterinary launch and met the two veterinary boatmen. They were particular friends of Ian's, as he had got them redesingnated as graded staff like drivers, so they got considerably more pay. As they travelled to Lamu Island, Ian pointed out another island called 'Manda', where there was an airstrip. He said the road journey up to Lamu was very laborious, so most people flew up. He made Katie and Suleiman laugh by saying, he thought Katie would prefer the luxury cruise. Katie put out her tongue at him. Suleiman said he had never done the trip by boat, but he would certainly try it, now he saw how she had enjoyed it!

The veterinary office was near to the jetty so they walked down to see the office staff before walking up to make a courtesy call on the DC. Katie noticed that it was a lovely old Arab town with some Portuguese influence. The Portuguese fort had been made into a jail. The DC told Katie with a smile that they never ever had any prisoners!

As it was getting near to lunch time they went to the hotel called 'Petley's' which was also on the waterfront. It had four stories. The ground floor seemed to be for storage, the next floor was the bar and eating area, the one above was the six bedrooms; the roof was for the more adventurous guests, as it was a totally open flat roof. Beds were brought up as required by guests. Ian ordered a bed for them. Katie was relieved that they seemed to be the only guests. Curry lunch was washed down with a couple of beers and then they went to their bed which was under an awning, for a siesta. The bed was not actually overlooked so they both stripped off. There was a slightly breeze which made the temperature bearable. Ian could not keep his hands off a nude Katie who tried to stop him saying she felt shy, but very soon succumbed to his advances. They spent a very pleasant early afternoon, before going for a walk north from the waterfront towards the tiny village of Shella. Past Shella was the most beautiful remote beach where they could swim naked which Katie loved, before sitting under a palm tree having some ice cold lime juice which Ian had brought in a thermos. Katie smirked,

"I'm allowed a cold drink now? Is this to make me hot?" Ian replied,

“You sitting naked outside really turns me on?” She replied,

“So I can see!” She then came and sat in his lap. Then when they were really hot they went for another swim. It was just getting dark as they got back to ‘Petley’s’. Katie made her way to the loo as Ian went to the bar to get them two beers. The proprietor, called Darkie had made his appearance. He greeted Ian and just as Katie came into the room asked if they would be comfortable. Katie laughed,

“Certainly, I love your upstairs long-drop. I have never seen one of those before.” Darkie replied,

“I pride myself that it is the only one in the country. I can assure you it is an idyl rumour that it goes through the kitchens!” Katie replied,

“I'm pleased to hear that. What have you got for supper?” Darkie pretended to look for a menu but gave up and said,

“Fish curry.”

It was lovely and Katie was relieved that it was relatively mild. The rice was perfect and she was amazed with all the little side dishes; chopped banana, chopped tomato, chopped onion, grated coconut, and cut chillies. She left the later well alone.

Ian had learnt his lesson from the previous evening and they only had two tuskers. They were soon up on the roof lying on the bed which was positioned in the middle of the roof and therefore was not over looked. They could see the stars. There was no electricity on the island and so there was no extraneous light to spoil the night sky.There were some hurricane lights in the hotel, but they were soon extinguished. They had a torch in case they need to go down to loo in the night. It was not quite as cool as on the boat, but it was not hot. There was a slight breeze which had got up. Katie whispered,

“I don't want you to fall off the roof but could we move the bed slightly so this breeze is blowing directly up our bodies from our feet?” Ian could not see the point, but he obliged her. She then lay with her knees bent and her feet flat on the bed with her legs as wide apart as possible. Then she directed his hand to her bush, whispering,

“Could you just play with my pubic hair? Yes that’s it. It is very exciting for me in this breeze. Soon to Ian’s pleasure, Katie was moving her bottom up and down in almost frenzy and then her legs went straight and she gave a sharp intake of breath and lay panting. She murmured,

“Thank you. That was quite something.” Ian kissed her,

“I didn't really do anything,”

“I think my body is very strange. Your gentle hand and the breeze sent me right over the top.” When she calmed down she said,

“I've been meaning to ask you. Shatri told me that his two wives are friends! How weird is that? I'm not a jealous girl, but I don't think I could be friends with a girl who was your sexual partner. What do you think?” Ian sighed,

“I'm sorry I can't help you there. It is totally beyond my experience. I certainly don't want to share you with anyone. I could no more go to a wife swopping party than fly around the moon. Let's just enjoy the moon together.”

Sure enough the almost full moon was rising above the neighbouring buildings. They languidly made love.

There was no rush in the morning, as the cattle which they had examined the day before, had walked down slowly from Burgoni and were not due to be loaded until noon. So Ian and Katie had a lazy morning on the beach before being picked up by the veterinary launch. Bonanza set sail at two. Either Katie had got used to the smell or the motion of the ship dissipated it, but she enjoyed sunbathing while Ian sat in a chair writing rather boring reports.

Once agin Ian did not drink too much at supper and so there was some lively love making before they both slept like logs. At KMC, Ian gave Katie a lift to the aero club at the airport so she could have a shower and get into her uniform. They walked together to the terminal. Ian was pleased to meet all the rest of Katie’s crew. They had enjoyed their time at the ‘Oceanic Hotel’, but the girls were amazed to hear Katie's experiences. They obviously thought she was totally mad. Katie did not know whether they guessed that she and Ian were lovers, but she suspected they did. They definitely would have guessed, if they had seen that she had stuffed all her dirty washing in his bag.

The next stop over in Nairobi was unexpected. The crew arrived at the ‘Panafric Hotel’ at breakfast time on a Saturday morning. Katie rang Ian who was delighted that she had arrived. He was just on his way to work which he knew would be a series of boring meetings, so Katie said she would stay at the ‘Panafric Hotel’ with the rest of the crew and see him at the rugby game. Although in theory it was an away game, 'Nondes' were playing 'Impala' who were another Nairobi side, so Ian gave Katie directions to get to the pitch.

Katie and the rest of the girls had an enjoyable morning by the pool. When they were eating lunch, Nicola asked Katie if she would mind if she came to the rugby game. Katie said that would be fine. The other eight girls thought they would enjoy seeing thirty fit young men playing, so eventually all the girls went in a minibus to 'Impala'. They had all got out of their uniforms and made a real effort with their turnout and so they caused a real stir when they arrived at the pitch. Katie briefed them that they must support 'Nondes' who would be playing in white. The opposition, 'Impala' would be playing in red. Katie met up with Jean and the twins. Jean said,

"Well done Katie bringing all these supporters. 'Nondes' need all the support they can get as they have not beaten 'Impala' at home for three years." Katie replied,

"I have told the girls who they are supporting. They are used to being a team themselves, so I think they will do a lot of shouting."

Sadly although the girls did a lot of cheering, 'Impala' were much the stronger side and they were well ahead in the closing minutes. 'Nondes' had not even scored a point. Katie shouted to Nicola,

"This is disastrous we must do something."

The play moved over to their side of the pitch. Nicola had idea and shouted,

"Knickers off girls. We will wave them to give our boys some encouragement."

So off came their knickers and they waved them enthusiastically. On the whole the majority of the crowd were men. Regardless as to whom they actually supported a massive cheer went up. Ian was not the 'Nondes' Captain but he was the pack leader. He shouted to the 'Nondes' pack,

"Come on lads, these ten girls have come all the way from the UK. Let's show them what we can do."

With the girls waving their knickers and Ian shouting at his forwards they seemed to have a new lease of life. They won the line-out and made short work of the 'Impala' back row and crashed over for a try. In fact they even managed a second try before the final whistle went. ‘Impala’ had won by a good margin, but at least it had not been a white-wash.

There was a great party after the game. Katie and Ian never did find out which of the girls put their knickers back on and indeed which of the girls ‘pulled’ that night. However in the Landrover on the way home in the dark, Ian slid his hand up under her skirt and said,

“You seem to have lost your knickers. Will I get lucky tonight?” She laughed and said,

“You will if you get us home in one piece. They were one of my favourite pairs so I put them safely in my handbag.”

They had a most enjoyable weekend. Now Katie really felt she was part of the crew and although she was sad leaving Ian she was glad to see the girls on Monday evening at Embakasi.

Chapter 6

Hijack

Ian was just about to take off from the LMD holding ground at Mukogodo near Isiolo when he saw three khaki clad figures waving and running towards him. He guessed they were from the British Army Training Team which had been based up in the NFD for some years.

Ian throttled back and cut the engine. He got out of the Cherokee Arrow by sliding across the passenger seat, as it had only a single door. Jumping down off the wing he waited for the three men who he saw were carrying a Bergen each and other kit. He asked as they came up,

"How can I help?" The leader, called Sid, recognised him,

"You're the vet; can you give us a lift, we are needed in Nairobi urgently? I'm Sid and this is Greg and Archie." Ian said,

"Not a problem, we are low and I don't have much stuff. Put your kit in the back. You just caught me."

So they set off, heading for Nairobi. Once they were airborne Sid said to Ian,

"Have you made a flight plan?"

"Not yet. I was going to make an airborne one, when we were higher."

"Do you mind not making one? There is a hijack on a BOAC VC10. The hijackers maybe tuned in." Ian suddenly started to worry. What if Katie was on that plane? He tried to relax. The likelihood was not great, but it was possible. Ian replied,

"Certainly, where should we aim for? I imagine you want to go to Eastleigh?" Sid replied,

"No we are a separate group. That's why they haven't sent a chopper for us. Can you land on the taxiway round to the North of the terminal at the main airport? We will just get out and leave you. You can then take off in a Northerly direction and swing round West and come in to Wilson in the normal manner."

Ian nodded but he was thinking. Then he said,

"My help comes at a cost." Sid looked at him shrewdly,

"My guess is that it is not money you are after. I know quite a lot about you. It is part of my brief to know what is happening in the NFD. What do you want?"

"Simple," Replied Ian. "I want to join your team."

"Sorry Ian, but that's just not possible. You have no training."

"Maybe not, but I have other attributes. I'm fluent in Swahili and I speak a bit of Masai. I think and can behave like a tribesman. You are going to need a plan and some guile, if you are going to spring this hijack. I may just be able to help you. You have nothing to loose. At the end of the day, I will disappear off to the NFD and no one will be any the wiser."

"Thanks for the offer, but I have got to say. No. Why do you want to risk your neck? We are doing it because it is our job."

"I have a girl friend who is an air hostess. If she were on that plane I would like to give her the best chance of survival. Anyhow I will get you to Embakasi as quickly as possible. Just remember my offer."

They flew on. Sid talked to some senior guy on some prearranged radio frequency. Ian listened. It sounded if these three were SAS, but they were in Kenya by chance. The whole scenario was being handled by the Kenyan Special Forces. Neither the senior guy nor Sid was happy with this arrangement, but it sounded as if their hands were tied.

Ian was actually taking quite a risk coming into Embakasi without clearance, but he thought, '*I'm sure I will be able to talk my way out of trouble.*'

As soon as they landed, Sid and his mates jumped out and taking their kit disappeared in to the massive aviation fuel depot. All Sid said was,

"Thanks Ian you've been a star. I will get some big cheese to allow you to take off again. Just wait here."

Ian waited. A couple of Africans who worked for Shell wandered over. They told Ian that there was chaos everywhere at the airport. They said that a VC10 was on route from Johannesburg and had been hijacked. Initially the Kenyan authorities would not let it land so in had circled until it was almost out of fuel. Then it had been allowed to land, but the plane had just sat on the Tarmac. No one had gone anywhere near it.

Katie was on the flight. She was with her normal girls, but on the flight deck was the senior captain, called Algernon who had been in charge on her very first long haul flight. Katie had not really been very bothered by his presence. He was just a reminder of the past. She had matured since then. She had made her friends and the pilots on long haul did not tend to socialise that much, so she had no actual problems. They just nodded at one another. After take off, Katie had made sure she took them their supper on the flight deck. She did not want them to think she was scared of them. In fact they were all quite civil to her.

The hijackers had taken over the plane after the cabin lights had been turned out. They were four men all dressed in smart suits. Somehow they had got four pistols on board together with some explosive device which the leader claimed he could trigger at any moment. The leader and another hijacker had burst on to the flight deck. The leader sat down in the spare seat, nicknamed the jump seat, and pointed a gun at the navigator across from him. The other man held a gun at the captain's head.

All the passengers at this stage were unaware of the drama. The first class had been empty, but for these four men. When the leader and the other man had gone on to the flight deck the other two men had gone into the first class kitchen area and now held Katie and Yvonne, the senior hostess at gun-point.

Katie could not really understand herself. She was, not only unafraid, but also was hyper-aware of her surroundings. She thought, *'I'm pleased that bastard of a senior captain is on board. He probably is the best man to handle this.'*

On the flight-deck the leader made his demands to the senior captain. Katie was correct. Algernon probably was the best man to handle the situation. Somehow he alerted the co-pilot and the navigator, as he casually switched off the auto-pilot. Then he suddenly yanked the stick to the left and kicked on left rudder with his foot. The hijacker with the gun at his head lost his footing and the co-pilot tried to grab his arm. There was a shot. The leader had calmly shot the navigator in the head and levelled his gun at the co-pilot and fired again. The co-pilot had been hit in the chest and slumped on to floor, groaning. The leader levelled his gun at Algernon, saying,

"You see I mean business. Kindly get the plane straight and level."He turned to the other hijacker, "Get into the co-pilot's seat. Bloody well kill this idiot if he tries anymore tricks!"

Algernon was a brave man. Initially he got the plane straight and level. Then he put his hands in his lap and said,

"I'm not doing anymore, until you let me summon one of the cabin staff to render first aid to my co-pilot."

The leader was a shrewd man. He did not want to shoot the captain. His bluff had been called. He said,

"Very well you can get someone."

A lot had happened in the aircraft. Yvonne had snapped on the seat belt sign and still at gun-point had grabbed the tannoy and told the passengers to remain seated, as they were experiencing severe turbulence. Katie had switched on all the cabin lights and grabbed the phone to flight deck. Shouting into it,

"There is a hijack!"

The hijacker nearest to her had knocked the internal phone out of her hand. Levelling his gun at point blank range at her, he said,

"One more stunt like that Blondie and you're history. Anyway the pilot already knows. The others are already on the flight deck."

Katie made a mental note that these two were the only hijackers with the passengers. Then the internal telephone bleeped. Katie just looked at the man who had hit her hand. He said,

"Go ahead and answer it, but no tricks." He pushed the gun into her tummy with a leer. Katie calmly picked up the phone and said,

"Yes Captain, this is Katie in the first class kitchen. What do you require?"

"Could you come on to the flight deck and render medical assistance to my co-pilot."

Katie's heart sank. She had heard the two shots. Contrary to popular belief, a shot from a small bore pistol does not automatically cause decompression on an aircraft flying at altitude. She told the two hijackers what the Captain had requested. One kept his gun on

Yvonne and the other indicated that Katie should go forward and he followed. Katie grabbed a small first aid box and went to the flight deck with him behind her. She knocked on the door and the Captain called,

"Come in."

She was not prepared for the sight which was before her. She instantly knew the navigator was dead, and she saw, and heard the co-pilot on the floor. She knelt beside him in the very cramped compartment, hyper-aware of the gun held by the leader right beside her. Before she could say anything the leader made a sign to the hijacker behind her and he closed the door. Her first thought was to help the co-pilot, but she also wanted to inform the Captain how many hijackers there were. She snapped at the leader,

"I need space to examine him. Can you get your two men in the first class kitchen to move him into the first class cabin? There is no one else in there."

The Captain was grateful for the information and wanted to indicate to Katie to be very careful. He guessed she already knew that, but wanted to encourage her.

"Thank you Katie. I know you are the youngest of my crew but you are the best. Your behaviour in the NFD confirms that." He turned to the leader,

"Please do as she asks." The leader calmly said,

"Very well, but I will move the man. No tricks young lady. You can see that I know how to use this gun." He put it in his belt and helped Katie move the co-pilot, who seemed to be unconscious. Katie ripped open his shirt and applied a large dressing to the bullet hole which was bleeding profusely. She felt under him and could not feel an exit hole. She decided not try and bandage him, but to apply pressure herself.

"I will have to hold this until the bleeding is less. However I think he is dying, but you bloody well don't care."

"You are wrong young lady. Katie isn't it?" Katie nodded, thinking, '*Somehow I think it is important to have a rapport with this guy.*' He continued,

"Your Captain was very foolish. I had no choice." Katie then realised that the co-pilot had stopped breathing. She felt his neck for a pulse. There was none. She said flatly,

“He’s died. I will cover him with blankets. You had better help me move the dead navigator out of here and I will cover him as well. If the passengers see dead bodies they will panic.”

“Katie, you are very calm for one so young.” Katie could not control her anger any more and spat back,

“I’ve been trained.”

Once the bodies were covered without asking, Katie walked on to the flight deck,

“Captain, would you like your usual coffee, or shall I add some sugar?”

“Thank you Katie. Yes I think I need some sugar. Sorry for everything.” Katie smiled at him to tell him she had forgiven him, not only for the incident months ago, but also for causing the deaths of these two men. She did not offer coffee to the hijackers.

When she got to the first class galley, she found Nicola as well as Yvonne with guns pointing at them. Nicola had obviously come forward to find out what was happening. Katie asked,

“Is everything OK further back? I've come back to get the Captain a coffee.” Before Nicola could reply one of the men snapped,

“No more talking.” Katie snapped back,

“I was asked to bring a report back for the Captain.” This was a complete lie, but Katie knew the more information he had the better. She poured the coffee and left them.

Back on the flight deck the atmosphere was electric. The leader had made the Captain call Nairobi to ask permission to land. The Captain had used some secret code, known only to BOAC that he had been hijacked. Initially Nairobi had granted permission, but then that was rescinded and a request was given asking for the reason. The leader would not let the Captain answer. Katie had heard nothing of this interchange, but twigged that something had happened. She gave the Captain his coffee saying,

“Yvonne and Nicola are in the first class galley. The rest of the plane is quiet.”

“Thank you Katie.” Katie had not finished. She turned to the hijacker in the co-pilots seat saying,

“You had better let me sit there. I will need to fly the plane to give the Captain a break.”

The Captain did not show any surprise, but thought, '*I totally underestimated this girl. I was a bloody fool.*"

The hijacker looked at the leader who just nodded. He then got up. Katie sat in the co-pilots seat and he sat in the navigator's seat.

The Captain said,

"Thanks Katie I could do with a breather. Nairobi has refused us permission to land so we will have to circle to the South of the zone. I will have to tell the staff and the passengers." He turned to the leader, who had now changed places, so he was pointing his gun at Katie. He just nodded,

"No tricks or Katie dies!"

The pilot marvelled at her composure. She did not bat an eyelid, but calmly took the stick in her right hand and covered his hand on the four throttles with her left hand. The Captain removed his hand, but not before he had given hers a brief unseen stroke. The Captain announced over the tannoy, that they were circling over Kenya to burn up some fuel before landing to get a minor problem with the instruments sorted out. He turned and looked briefly at Katie, as she pretended to fly the aircraft. In reality she just let it fly itself, as the Captain had secretly flipped on the autopilot. Both of them were frantically trying to think what they could do. The leader took this opportunity to tell the Captain his demands. He required ten million dollars in used large denomination notes and a helicopter to take him and his men to an unknown destination. The Captain leant back in his seat and pretended to sleep.

Katie's mind was in overdrive. She thought what a fool she had been to put herself forward to be directly in the firing line. Then she thought she was really in the front line anyway in the first class galley. At least being here she knew to some extent what was happening. There was really nothing she could do at the moment. She would just have to bide her time. She could then see how it all panned out. She thought with fondness of Ian. She really wasn't far away from him. She imagined him still sleeping. She so wished she was cuddled beside him. She longed for his hands to gently caress her. She did not despair. She was determined she was going to survive and that she was going to save as many of the passengers and the crew as possible.

The hours went by. The hostesses were rushed off their feet seeing to breakfast as they were down three girls, as the hijackers would not let Nicola return to the cabin. There were always two hijackers so that they could let Nicola or Yvonne leave to go to the loo. Equally both Katie and Algernon were allowed to the lavatory.

The Captain eventually persuaded Nairobi tower to let him land as he was getting low on fuel. Katie pretended she was helping, but in fact she had to do very little. The tower ordered them to park on the side beside the main runway. Then there was a stalemate. The leader would not let anyone near the plane. The tower heard his demands and said they would pass them on. They just sat there getting hotter and hotter. The Captain took his jacket and tie off. Katie took off her jacket and cravat. She felt sweat running down between her breasts and remembered laughing with Ian about girls only getting hot. She was certainly hot now. There were only two small windows.

Then Felicity from the back of the cabin came on the line. She told the Captain that the passengers were complaining about the heat and wanted to know what the delay was.

The Captain looked at the leader, who said,

"Tell them there are some minor electrical problems. Then get on to Nairobi tower and tell them that I will started executing the passengers in groups of five in half an hour and then at half hourly intervals until my demands are met."

On the ground the Kenyan Special Forces were planning to storm the plane. The British High Commission was trying to stop them until a full squad of the SAS had arrived from RAF Cyprus. Sid was at his wits end, as he did not know what to do. The High Commissioner knew of his presence, but would not let him take any action. All Sid knew was there were four hijackers demanding money. Ian also did not know what to do until he suddenly had an idea, when he saw a mob of Masai cattle just outside the perimeter fence. He got a message to Sid using the Shell men to take a note.

Sid came out to the plane,

"I thought you were going to bugger off?" Ian replied,

"I have an idea."

"Well you had better tell me. I have no ideas myself. I have been studying plans of VC10s until I can no longer think straight. We are waiting for a squad of SAS, but the Kenyans want to mount an attack. The hijackers are threatening to kill some passengers." Ian asked,

"Do you know how many hijackers there are?"

"No but the rumour is there are four, as there were four possible candidates and they were the total number in the first class. The other bookings in the first class appear to be bogus."

"Well my plan is simple. We four blacken ourselves and dress like Masai. We cut the perimeter fence out of sight of the plane. I persuade a group of Masai to let us help drive their cattle on to the airfield and under the plane. We get up into the plane via the wheels and the Masai keep driving their herd onwards. Once we are in the plane we eliminate the hijackers. End of story!"

Sid scratched his head,

"Well it is simple. It sounds infinitely better than the Kenyans trying to rush the plane with passenger ramps. I'll get the others and we will give it a go."

So they got ready after Sid had cleared the plan with the High Commissioner. The tower knew nothing of the plan, but were told to keep stalling as best they could, saying they were having difficult getting the cash.

Algernon and Katie were getting frantic on the flight deck. Yvonne had brought coffee and soft drinks, but the hijackers were getting impatient. Katie tried to reason with the leader, saying how she knew Africa well and everything always took a long time. The leader listened, but he started losing his cool particularly, when one of his men from the cabin came and told him about a herd of cattle. He calmed down a bit, when he, himself, saw them all move off. Katie said totally innocently, "See what I mean. This is Africa." The leader said,

"Tell the tower, time is up the first five passengers will die in five minutes."

As this message was being relayed, the door burst open. The leader took Sid's bullet in the head and the other hijacker was stunned by Ian's Masai '*rungu*' (a cosy made from a strong stick with a large iron nut screwed on to its end).

Katie did not recognise him until he spoke.

"Four hijackers accounted for. Are there any more?"

"No my darling, there were only four." The Captain was flabbergasted.

"Is this your boy friend?" Katie replied laughing with relief,

"What did you think, you silly bugger, that this guy is part of a Masai raiding party!"

Sid was searching the leader for any other weapons or explosive devices. Ian did the same to the other hijacker. Their guns appeared to be their only weapons. The Captain was on the radio calling for the steps to be brought up, not only with more back up to secure the three hijackers which were still alive, but also to evacuate the passengers. Katie went to help the other girls. Sid checked that the leader was definitely dead and dragged the other hijacker in to the first class and watched to make sure he was securely handcuffed by the Kenyan troops.

The Captain offered his hand to Ian saying,

"I'm Algernon Cavendish. Your Katie was marvellous. I should have known she was in the top flight when I first met her. I was her first Captain." Ian scowled,

"You're the bastard who tried to assault her at the 'Panafric' Hotel'. She seems to have forgiven you. You are lucky or I would have beaten you over the head." Then Ian was silent for a second before adding,

"Well I suppose I should thank you, as I would never have met her if you hadn't been such a bastard. If you're ever nasty to her again, God help you!" Katie had come on to the flight deck. She put her hand on Ian's shoulder,

"Uck, this boot black is revolting. I'm not showering with you. I would end up looking like a zebra. I heard you warning Algy. I hope you have taken that to heart. CAPTAIN. However I have got to hand it to you. You did well today. I trust you will fix it so that I can have two weeks leave with this *Moran* (A term for a Masai Warrior). Algernon knew when he was on a loser and so he acquiesced with dignity. He knew that he also would get two weeks leave.

Chapter 7

Katie makes the most of the first of her two weeks leave

Katie said goodbye to the rest of the crew and walked with her '*Moran*' to the waiting Cherokee Arrow behind the terminal. They made a comical sight; a very elegant air hostess with a Masai wearing only a red blanket wheeling her airline case. What was really extraordinary was that the '*Moran'* flew the plane. Katie teased the '*Moran'* by looking under his red blanket and saying that she had a mind to send him back to his '*manyatta'* (a Masai house) as he was not as well endowed as she had expected.

Nelson was used to Ian's strange behaviour and so he did not comment on his attire but made them both a good supper which they washed down with a bottle of wine. As Katie was getting into bed, Ian came up behind her, pushed her on to the bed and lay on top of her holding her arms firmly on the bed.

"So your '*Moran*' is not well enough endowed for you." Katie did not answer but tried to wriggle out of his grasp. She immediately realised her mistake, as that aroused him more. She felt him hard between her thighs. She was very ticklish and so Ian started kissing her under her arms, on her neck and in her ears. In between giggles she managed to say,

"I was wrong; my '*Moran*' is surprisingly well endowed. I can feel his magnificent manhood." Her voice contained a lot of laughter and very little sincerity. She was rewarded with more tickling and she felt a hand between her thighs. She tried to keep them together but the hand was very persistent. Soon the fingers were doing wonderful things and the temptation to open her thighs was too great. Then she felt something that she certainly regretted belittling. It was very hard and moved rhythmically, in and out of her moist lips. She climaxed as she heard him give a deep sigh of satisfaction.

They had been apart for sometime and so she was very happy to get into bed and lie on her back and welcome him again. It was only when they were truly spent that they slept.

They were woken by Nelson bringing in the tea. He always brought it in to the bed-side table on Ian's side. This morning Ian was given a treat as Katie leaned across him to pour their teas. He buried his face in her breasts. She giggled,

"That face has got a lot of bristles. It must belong to a '*Moran*' with a very big manhood. I must have instinctively known that on the day we met and I felt this face on my thigh. So on balance we have got a lot to thank Algy for." She then added in a pretended wistful voice,

"I bet he has an enormous manhood." There was a growl from Ian. Their tea was cold by the time they drank it. Ian was not early for work. He left Katie still in bed. She was happily sunbathing in his garden, when he came home for lunch. It was only then that they made some plans for her two weeks stay.

The first plan was for a romantic meal out in Nairobi that evening. Katie pulled out all the stops and looked ravishing which is exactly what she got when they returned home. In the morning they drove up to some friends of Ian's, Simon and Alison, who had a ranch near Nanyuki. They arrived for an early lunch. Their hosts did not know Katie was coming but seemed very relaxed. Simon was slightly surprised that Katie, who he had been told was an air hostess, and in his opinion was stunning, came out in the afternoon to do the veterinary work. She was wearing short shorts and a low top. Her long legs were breath-taking. Simon could not keep his eyes of her and when she got in the middle seat of the Landrover he had great difficulty keeping his hands off her. She teased him saying,

"Don't worry. I quite enjoy having my right knee put into fourth gear. Ian is doing it all the time. What is even more fun is when he pulls the red nob backwards and rubs my inner thigh with his elbow." Simon was speechless.

Ian told her that their job that afternoon was to wash out twenty bulls. She asked,

"Have we got to wash out their mouths? I remember at Burgoni, just examining their tongues was quite laborious." Ian laughed,

“We are going to a different part of their anatomy. We have got to wash out each one’s prepuce.” Katie chuckled,

“That sounds fun. Will they mind?” Ian replied,

“No, I don't think they mind. In fact I think they quite enjoy it.”

Simon was now bright red in the face. Katie thought he was going to burst a blood vessel, when to tease him she said,

“Well I will wash them very gently and try to make it an enjoyable experience. I remember washing that boot black of your Willy, Ian that was a real mission. I was quite gentle then and you seemed to enjoy it.”

They arrived at the bull yard. As usual the animals were already in a big pen and there were several tall men standing around wearing very little. The first bull was got into the front of the race. It was a very large humped white animal. It seemed fairly docile to Katie. It was just its enormous size which was rather intimidating. She was pleased to see it didn't have any horns. She said to Ian,

“I will watch what you do with the first one and then I can help with the next one.”

The bull had a large pendulous prepuce. Ian grabbed it through the bars of the race. Then he asked Simon to tie a short length of white elastic bandage loosely around it, but not to tighten it. Ian then put a small bore plastic pipe into the prepuce. He squirted some oily antibiotic liquid up the tube. Holding the prepuce tightly he removed the tube and got Simon to tighten the bandage. He massaged the liquid as far as it would go back towards the scrotum. Katie who was watching carefully, said much to Simon’s embarrassment,

“What enormous balls. I bet you wish you had a pair like that Simon?” He mumbled some reply. Then she said,

“I'm sure I could do that if Simon will help me tie up the bandage?”

So they started work in two teams; Katie and Simon, Ian and the Headman.

Katie was a little monkey. She could see how embarrassed Simon was working close to her. As she was massaging the antibiotic oily liquid up high into the back of the prepuce she whispered,

“I like this job. I can feel the tip of his Willy. It is ever so hard. I think Ian’s right. He is enjoying it.”

So that was their afternoon job. It was finished when they removed the last bandage which had to stay on for a minimum of half an hour, so that all the potential organisms had been killed by antibiotics. When they were in the Landrover, Katie announced,

"We are all filthy and need a good shower. I think I smell worse that 'Bonanza'." Ian had to explain to Simon what she was talking about.

As with so many Kenyan properties, there was a quest house. Katie and Ian made themselves at home after they had enjoyed a long hot shower together. They then went up to the main house to have a beer before supper with Simon and Alison.

Alison asked them what they had been up to. Katie proceeded to tell her in graphic detail. Then she turned to Ian and asked,

"I think you are right. The bulls do enjoy it particularly the massaging bit. What confuses me is that you can feel their hard penis, but it seems too short to do anything useful!" Simon nearly choked on his beer. Ian explained that bulls have a different mechanism from humans. Their penis does not swell much, but has a large S bend, called a sigmoid flexure, which straightens out when they serve a cow. This way all ruminants which includes; cows, sheep, goats, deer and antelope, can be really quick and so lessen the danger of being caught by a lion. Katie retorted,

"I don't like the sound of this really quick business. I feel sorry for the cows. It wouldn't suit me!" Simon inhaled sharply and said,

"Let's go through for supper?"

It was a lovely meal. Katie got on really well with Alison. They weren't late to bed, as they knew they had a good lot of work to do in the morning.

Simon was in bed when Alison came through to come to bed. He remarked,

"Are you cold? You never normally wear pyjamas?" Alison smirked,

"I thought I would act on what Katie was saying about poor old cows. I expect you to take my pyjamas off very slowly and take some time. Hopefully you won't be eaten by a lion while you are doing it!"

In the morning they all had a good breakfast. Then Alison surprised Simon by saying,

"Can I come with you this morning? I would like to learn more about the cattle." Simon prevaricated,

"Really my dear, won't you get bored?" She replied,

"Katie doesn't seem to. I have learnt a lot from her already. I think you enjoyed going slower last night as much as I did!" After that Simon did not dare to argue with her.

When they got to the Landrover, Alison went to get in the back. Katie stopped her and got Ian to take the windows off the top of the doors. Then there was room for them all to sit abreast in the front. Alison had shorts on. She sat between Simon who was driving and the gear lever. Her thigh rubbing against him gave him an erection. She kissed him on his neck and said,

"I'm glad my thigh still excites you darling. I will wear shorts more often. This is really cosy." Katie added,

"Yes, I'm enjoying it. If you are the only passenger, you can put your left leg outside of the vehicle. Then you get a very erotic breeze up your shorts."

"Wow that sounds a good tip."

The morning's job was doing vasectomies on twenty young bulls. They could not work in two teams, as Ian was the only surgeon. So they worked in a group. The young bull was given a strong sedative injection in its rump. When it lay down on its side, Simon held its upper hind leg and Katie washed its scrotum. Once again she said she enjoyed that job. Alison held the little tray with the syringes and local anaesthetic. Ian then injected both areas where he was going to make his incisions. Then Katie cleaned the scrotum surgically. After Ian had scrubbed his hands, he made a small incision in the skin over the spermatic chord on the lower testicle. He could now see the vas deferens in the cord. He grasped it with forceps before removing an inch of it. He put in a couple of sutures in the skin. Then they rolled the bull over and repeated the procedure on the other side. The bull was then allowed to lie there until it was strong enough to get up. They stopped for a picnic lunch and continued until they were all finished.

On the way back to the ranch, Alison wanted to sit on the outside, so that she could put her leg out of the window. She agreed with Katie that it was a very stimulating sensation. When they reached the ranch she dragged a bemused Simon into the house, shouting,

“See you for a drink before supper.” Simon thought, as he was enjoying a tea time romp that Katie’s visit had been excellent.

Both Alison and Simon were very sad to say goodbye to Katie in the morning!

As Katie was driving away from the ranch, Ian remarked,

“Katie it is such good fun working with you. You are so spontaneous! I think if I said, ‘How about a shag? You would stop the Landrover, jump out and pull your shorts and knickers off.’” To his amazement that's what she did!

They drove out of Nanyuki, as if they were going to the NFD, but before they dropped down towards Isiolo they turned right and continued on the sides of Mount Kenya to Meru. They made their way to the Meru Veterinary Office. Ian introduced Katie to the District Veterinary Officer (DVO), a very serious, earnest, man who was called Percy Higgins. He took one look at Katie and said,

“You won't want to do any veterinary work. We will take you up to my house first and you can stay with my wife.” Katie smiled sweetly,

“That's really kind of you. I will enjoy meeting your wife later, but I would like to do some veterinary work first.” Percy replied,

“I don't think it would be proper as the tribesmen wear very little.” Katie was feeling devilish and replied,

“That’s no problem Percy; I can easily take off my clothes if that would be more proper so the tribesmen won't be upset.” Percy was at a loss. He opened his mouth twice and then decided not to say anything, but just grunted.

So they set off in Percy’s Landrover. Katie sat in the middle seat and asked Percy all about his District. Percy then realised she was not a dumb blond, but very intelligent and what was more she was genuinely interested in the country with its people and their animals. He told her that he was lucky as his District was very varied. The highest point, Mount Kenya, was snow and rock. Below that was high altitude open grassland which was very boggy, but had beautiful wild flowers. Lower down was the forest which contained a large number of different species of game including the ‘Big Five’, but also some rare species like Giant Forest Hog and elusive different species of Duiker. The land below the forest was farmed by the Meru People who were closely related to the biggest tribe in Kenya, the

Kikuyu. High up they grew coffee, lower down they had dairy cows and grew, maize, pyrethrum, cabbages, green beans and potatoes. As you descended the rainfall dropped and so they kept beef cattle which required more and more land area per animal the lower you descended. Lowest of all was the so called 'Hot Country' where there were Tsetse flies. This area was not suitable for farming as the cattle would die of Trypanosomiasis which was spread by the Tsetse fly. This part of his District was Meru Game Park. Katie asked him questions like; what breeds of cattle were there? Did they use AI? What species of game animals, etc. Percy realised he liked her and when he looked down at her bronze thighs he realised he liked her rather a lot!

Their destination was the 'Hot Country' just above the Tsetse area. Cattle had been dying and as yet the Veterinary Department did not know why. Percy had taken a large number of blood slides, blood samples and slides from the Lymph Nodes (LNs), but so far there was nothing definite. Today they were going to collect urine samples. These would be injected into hamsters which Kabete had sent up. They would then have to be taken to the laboratory as quickly as possible. Katie said,

"I feel a bit sorry for the hamsters. I would not like urine injected into me." Percy agreed with her.

Eventually they arrived at a cattle race and crush with cattle, men and boys milling about. There was a general meeting with lots of talk and waving of arms. Percy was despondent as there were neither recently dead animals nor any sick animals. They had had a wasted journey. Katie was not part of the meeting and was standing in the shade of a large Acacia tree when a very tall man, carrying two spears joined her. He had just a thin strip of cloth over his shoulder. She tried out her Swahili. She said,

"Hello. How was he?" He replied,

"He was very well. How was she?" Katie replied,

"She was very well. How were his cattle?" He answered,

"Two are very sick." Katie asked,

"Are they near?" He replied,

"Yes, I will show you." He led her by the hand off into the bush. Katie thought,

‘*This is a novel experience.*’ It never occurred to her that she was in any danger. They walked for several hundred yards and eventually came to three other men clad in a similar manner with two, ill looking cows. Katie tried her Swahili again,

“Would he send one of his friends to bring the European men and their bags of medicine here?” He nodded. There was a conversation in a language quite different from Swahili and one man went back the way they had come. Katie’s new friend and the two other men then rested on their hunches. They had their feet flat on the ground and their knees bent and their legs a little apart. Katie was wearing quite a short skirt but thought it would be rude not to join them. So she squatted down. She knew she was giving anyone who cared to look a good view of her rather small pair of knickers. She was slightly miffed that no one cared to look! She had a difficult job not looking at the men! She thought she ought to show some interest so she asked,

“Had they many cattle?”

“Yes they had many cattle.”

“We're any others sick?”

“No, there were no others sick.”

“Had any died?”

“Yes, two had died.” Katie felt a little like being at a party and trying to make conversation to some one who she had never met before, but she soldiered on asking the age of the cows. She remembered the word for mouth and the word for tongue. Apparently neither was sore. She also remembered the word for blood. Apparently there had been blood. She asked was the blood from the mouth. Apparently the blood was not from the mouth. She pointed at her nose. Apparently the blood was not from the nose. She stood up, hitched up her skirt and pointed at her groin. All three men nodded enthusiastically. It was at this moment when a very red-faced Percy arrived. Katie turned to him lowering her skirt and said,

“Are there you are Percy, apparently they have had two which died with blood either in their urine or from their uterus. I didn't know the Swahili for vulva so I had to point. These two are sick.” The blood seemed to drain from Percy’s face. He managed,

“I see. Well done. I was worried about you.”

Ian then arrived and took over the consultation. Blood smears were taken, LNs in front of the shoulder were aspirated and blood samples were taken. Then Ian and Percy tried to get urine samples. They failed. Katie said,

"You hold the bottle. Let me try."

She put her index finger just inside the vulva and rubbed gently. She whistled softly and was rewarded by a dribble of urine. Her new friend who was holding the cow's tail, smiled. He held the second cow's tail and Katie repeated the procedure and was once again successful. Then there was a palaver as Ian and Percy injected the urine into four hamsters. Katie's new friend looked totally bemused. She left Ian to explain. Then both cattle were given injections of Oxytetracycline into their veins. The men were told that a veterinary scout would come the next day and repeat the injections. They went back to the Landrover, but not before the four men had shaken Katie by the hand in the African manner, grasping her little hand in both of their enormous hands. Percy was quiet on the drive home. Eventually he said,

"Katie, weren't you frightened with those four men in the bush on your own?"

She replied,

"No not at all. They seemed like nice chaps. I wish I could have spoken their language as it was a rather stilted conversation in a language which was a second language for both of us."

No more was said.

Katie was starving when they reached the Veterinary Office, as it was late afternoon. They were given cups of tea and some biscuits. Then Percy insisted that they come and stay with him and his wife. Ian volunteered for them to stay at the local Inn called the 'Pig and Whistle' but Percy was adamant.

Percy's wife whose name was Florence was totally flummoxed by their arrival. Their maid Ethel was immediately instructed to make up the bed in the spare room. Then Florence realised that they weren't married. She cried,

"Oh my goodness, that won't do at all. Can you sleep on a camp bed, Ian, in the sitting room? We only have one bath. How are you all going to get washed?" Katie then took charge,

“Florence, we will be fine in one bed. Ian is very well behaved. He doesn't snore, he doesn't wriggle about. In fact he is a perfect paragon of virtue. All we need is a bucket of warm water. Ian will rig up our camp shower on that big tree in your garden. You have no need to worry. We will be fine.” Percy thought he should help to reassure his wife,

“My dear, Katie is totally used to bush life. She even used her own body to find out from four tribesmen where blood was coming from their cows. She will be totally relaxed stripping off in the garden. It is not as if it is overlooked!” Florence shrieked,

“Percy, have you gone insane. I can’t have a white girl naked showering in my garden.” Katie could see that Percy was no helping. Equally she knew if she suggested that she and Ian went to the’Pig and Whistle’ that would be a slight on Florence's hospitality. So Miss KK went into bossy mode,

“Percy can you help Ian to get our things in from the Landrover. Florence, can you and I make a cup of tea. I don't know about you but I'm dying for one.” Before Florence could object, Katie whisked her into the kitchen in the way she had been taught to deal with difficult passengers. Once they were alone, Katie explained that she and Ian would be showering in their swimming costumes. She said that were like overgrown kids and loved playing with water in the garden. She explained that she had three elder brothers and so she treated Ian just like one of her brothers. She said she had been trained in the old fashioned way at BOAC and you just had to be very firm with men and then they behaved sensibly. Florence seemed to accept this. She was ready to accept that Katie would take charge of Ian. Having never had children and being of a different generation, she obviously let Percy make all the decisions in her life.

Katie enjoyed her cup of tea and then managed to get Ian into the spare bed room. She briefed him on the showering arrangements. They were to wear swimming costumes. There was to be no touching and certainly NO hankie pankie!

In fact the evening went off very well. Katie knew in Percy’s eyes she could do no wrong and Ian laid on all the charm for Florence.

Because they knew they should not make love, Katie and Ian both really felt like it. Katie took off her clothes in a very sexy manner in front of Ian. Then she rubbed herself with one hand while squeezing her breasts with the other. At the same time she kept licking her lips. When they went to get into bed, Katie could hardly contain herself as the bed squeaked. She whispered to him,

"You will have to pretend you are a bull with a sigmoid flexure. No time for fore-play you will have to be quick before a lion eats you."

With that she threw a towel on the floor and knelt on it with her forearms taking her weight so her bottom was delightfully up in the air for him. Ian was not frantic, so he got a pillow off the bed for her to put her face in and then proceeded to bring her to ecstasy with his hand. By then he was extremely excited and he was like a bull. One thrust and he came deep inside her, as she bit into the pillow. They lay together on the towel before very carefully getting into bed. Katie lay on her back and brought his face to her breasts. He sucked them gently and then they both slept. She was woken at dawn by him sucking her again. She whispered,

"Bloody Hell, have you been sucking them all night? I will come into milk like a maiden goat. Let me kiss you properly."

She cupped his rough chin in her hand and pushed her tongue deep into his mouth. She broke off the kiss when she felt his hand between her thighs, and whispered.

"I'm bursting for a wee. You had better stop or I might be like one of those cows yesterday."

They went in a relay to the loo and then got dressed and sat on the veranda. The view of Mount Kenya was spectacular.

Florence produced an excellent breakfast. Then Ian and Katie said their goodbyes and they set off to Meru Game Park. Ian had met the famous 'George Adamson' briefly before when George had got him to remove a grass seed which had lodged in 'Elsa's' ear. He had made Ian promise he would visit him again, if he was in the vicinity. Ian explained to Katie that George and Joy Adamson no longer saw eye to eye and so they lived either side of a crocodile infested river which suited them both. George lived inside a lion proof stockade and the lions lived outside. The lions were free to go wherever they liked. It was George who was in a cage like an animal in a zoo.

They arrived at the compound and George came out to meet them and ushered them in for a cup of coffee. Katie could not stop herself from looking behind her to check that a lion was not following her into the compound! George was obviously pleased to meet Katie in her short skirt and chatted about the game in Meru Game Park. He then suggested they went for a walk. He said he had not seen any lions for two days. He said he knew 'Elsa' was off somewhere having her cubs. He turned to Katie and said,

"Ian knows the form but the important thing if we meet a lion, particularly if it is 'Boy', is that you stand still and don't make any sudden movements. I always tell men to put their hands in their pockets but you haven't got any in that pretty skirt, so I should just cross your arms over your chest."

It was very exciting walking in a game park. Katie knew that none of her crew had ever done anything like this. George was a fountain of information about the birds and animals which they saw. They walked along the river which was indeed full of hippos and crocs. Katie thought, *'No chance of meeting Joy Adamson!'* She was wrong they did actually see her across the river. She waved and they waved back.

Suddenly a fully grown enormous male lion, bounded out of the bush. It came straight to George who fondled its ears. Then it seemed to recognise Ian as it rubbed its face on his legs. Katie was terrified, but she managed not to move her arms quickly and just slowly crossed them over her chest. The lion sniffed her ankles and slowly sniffed up her bare thighs. She was sweating. Lion slowly licked the sweat off her legs, working his way up her thighs. Katie thought, *'If I hadn't been so terrified this might be quite erotic. What is he going to do now?'* His nose and tongue went relentlessly up under her skirt. She thought, *'Bloody hell. I mustn't jump!'* Then he started licking the front of her knickers and between her legs. Slowly she reached down with her hands and fondled his ears. He started to purr and stopped licking, but he now rubbed his face on her thighs like he had done to Ian. He stopped, turned and bounded towards the compound. The three of them followed, but the lion went to what must have been his feeding place and they could get into the compound through the gate. George said,

"You did very well my dear. Many young ladies was have either jumped or squeaked which might have been disastrous. I'm sorry his tongue must be a little rough. Katie laughed and told George the story of Ian's face in the Landrover when she first met him. George thought that was hilarious and said,

"I imagine you didn't squeak then." Katie smiled,

"Funnily enough I didn't. I have been with him ever since!"

They were both sorry to leave George's camp and go to the Park HQ. However Katie had even larger members of the 'Big Five' to terrify her there. The Park Warden, James Howkins was a very old friend of Ian's. He was delighted to meet Katie. He said that he must apologise for their accommodation tonight, as he was a bachelor and lived a very Spartan existence. Katie tried to put him at his ease by saying,

"James, you mustn't worry about me. I think I can put up with anything. I've just had my fanny licked by a mature male lion. I'm sure your house will be fine." This made James splutter, as he certainly was not used to forth-right modern girls. To cover his embarrassment he said,

"Ian I'm sure you would like to get on with the work you have come to do. Katie would you like to have a cup of tea on my veranda and relax?" She replied with a smile,

"Ian has not briefed me on what he has come to do, but I'm sure I will want to participate?" James gulped and replied,

"Do you really want to do a rectal examination on a rhino?"

Katie was horrified at the prospect. However she was damned if she was going to admit it so she said,

"I have never done one before, but I hope I can make it a pleasurable experience for the rhino. I'm sure Ian will help me." It was Ian's turn to laugh,

"I have never done one before and I rather think no one else ever has either!" Katie was too frightened to add any more. As they got into James's Landrover, Katie thought, '*At least I can get this right. All men seem to like it, if I lift my right leg over the top of the gear lever and show them my knickers.*' She was certainly right in that assumption, as far as James was concerned.

They drove for about twenty minutes and James told them about the rhinos. Apparently there were no wild white rhinos left in Kenya although on the most recent estimates there were over eighty thousand black rhinos. Black rhinos should be called thin lipped rhinos as they were browsers. They were more aggressive than the thick lipped, often called white rhinos which were grazers. These white rhinos were a family group which had recently been imported from South Africa. There were two mature females and five younger animals. James wanted to know if the two mature females were pregnant and that's why he had asked Ian to come up. They were a fairly friendly group and were guarded constantly by two rangers who worked on a shift system.

When they arrived, the rhinos were grazing near a stockade which James had constructed. Although James said they were fairly benign, they appeared enormous to Katie. As she had recently been licked by a lion in her nether regions she certainly did not like the look of their two horns. The rhinos were all tempted into the stockade by some freshly cut maize. The two animals to be examined were much the biggest and were the most dominant. They used their bulk and horns to make sure they got the maize. There was some crashing about before one was persuaded to walk down the race after a particularly enticing maize stork. Large poles were then put behind her so that she could not reverse.

A bucket of water and some soap was produced. Ian took his shirt off. James looked at Katie expectantly. Katie rather vehemently shook her head. Ian soaped up his arm. As Ian was tall his shoulder was at the same height as the rhino's anus. One pole was removed from behind the rhino, so that Ian could reach forward and put his hand and then his whole arm up into the rhino's rectum. The rhino continued to eat the maize in front of it. With some delight Ian said,

"Good news James. I can feel a big calf in there." It was now time for Katie to show her metal. She soaped up her arm. A wooden box was brought for her to stand on, as she said to James to try to hide her nerves,

"Normally I work in high heals but I haven't brought any with me."

She plunged her arm into the rhino. It was quite a struggle, as the anus was tight and there seemed to be rather a lot of fairly dry dung. To the inexperienced Katie it just felt as if her arm was in a warm very thick soup. Then she felt something hard which seemed to kick out at her. With relief she exclaimed,

"I can feel a leg of a calf it moved!"

At that moment there was a commotion behind her as the second big animal had charged one of the smaller ones to stop it eating the maize. The crash of the smaller animal hitting the wall of the stockade spooked the rhino in the race. She clamped down her anus on Katie's arm above her elbow. Katie was trapped. Try as she might she could not pull her arm out,

"Ian, James help!"

Ian wrapped his arms around her from behind and pulled. James grabbed the soap and tried in vain to lubricate Katie's arm. In fact somehow her breasts in her low-cut top were massaged! Then Katie remembered collecting urine from the cows. She inserted a finger into the rhino's vagina and gently rubbed the mucosa. Katie heard the rhino give a grunt of satisfaction and the rhino relaxed her anal sphincter. Katie's arm came out like a cork from a bottle. She and Ian fell into the mud and dung in the race. Katie scrambled up out of the race showing all of her knickers to a delighted James, while Ian said,

"I don't think we need do the other one, James. It is pretty likely she is in calf!"

James's house although very basic did have a really good shower which was lucky as Ian and Katie were filthy. He offered them a cold beer but they both wanted a shower first. He was a little alarmed as he showed them to two rooms, but they both laughed and went together into one which was large, but only had a small single iron bed. Katie rocked it saying,

"At least it does not squeak. I could do with some serious, gentle, loving-making after today's, near death experiences. It is lucky I don't have nightmares or bad dreams. One would be of 'Boy' licking me to death, starting in my groin and the other would be having a rhino on the end of my arm for the rest of my days!"

James could not understand why they were taking so long to come for their cold beers. Supper was cottage pie and cabbage, followed by rice pudding and jam. Katie rather suspected that James had a similar supper every night! They were actually quite early to bed, as they were both exhausted. Katie made sure she was wrapped by a large arm which gently held one of her breasts and had her neck kissed as she drifted off to sleep.

They woke with a clatter of tea cups. Ian volunteered to bring her a cup of tea, but out of devilment she elected to wrap her self in a rather small threadbare towel which left little to the imagination and go and get their teas. Much to James' embarrassment she went to join him on the veranda and admire Mount Kenya in all its glory before it became covered in cloud. James found it very hard to relax and enjoy the view of the mountain. He was sure he would see the spectacular view again, but he regretted that he was unlikely to see the wonderful view beside him again. Eventually Katie stretched nearly losing her towel and announced,

"I had better take Ian his tea or he will take a stick to me." James was lost imaging such a sight.

They left after a great breakfast, which they guessed James had every morning, and headed for Embu. The 'Embu', Ian explained were a tribe closely related to the 'Kikuyu' and the 'Meru'.

All was well at the Veterinary Office. Dick Cladon took them home for lunch which was not popular with his very feisty wife, Lesley. She very quickly pointed out that the local hotel; the 'Isaac Walton' was very good. So after a rather makeshift lunch they repaired there to check in. They had a lovely chalet on their own with a veranda overlooking what looked like acres and acres of green grass which Ian told Katie were rice paddy fields, where they were going later in the afternoon. Katie enquired innocently whether they had time to try out the enormous feather bed. Ian said they probably could if they were quick. One look from her reminded him that speed was not what Katie had in mind! As always whenever she was in this sort of mood he had the most enjoyable afternoon.

Then they went duck shooting. Unknown to Ian, Katie had been taught how to use a shot gun and indeed a rifle at a very young age, by her brothers on the farm in the UK. They set off eastwards to the Mwea Rice Scheme. Ian talked eloquently about how good the shooting was. He said Katie must have a go, but she must be careful not to get a sore shoulder? Katie replied that she felt a little sorry for the ducks which had supplied them the most marvellous feather-bed and therefore would not shoot, but would watch him. Ian said the only real problem was retrieving the ducks after they had been shot. Katie said she would keep an eye out where they dropped. She made him promise not shoot more than four which they could get the hotel to cook for them for their supper.

When they reached the Rice Scheme they left the Landrover and walked along the straight narrow raised edges of the paddy fields. Katie did not think any duck would arrive until dusk, but she was wrong. One came over Ian and he shot it. It landed in the middle of a paddy field. He asked Katie,

"Can you retrieve it? I'm pretty certain it is dead. I will stay ready in case there is another one."

Katie then had to step off the dry path into the sticky mud of the paddy field which had been flooded to about a depth of a foot with water. Walking was difficult as the mud was very clingy. She reached the duck which was indeed dead and was floating on the surface. Ian then to his delight shot two duck, a left and a right. In his excitement he just shouted and waved his arms,

"Just twenty yards to your right. The other is thirty yards to your left."

Katie got the first of the pair, but could not see the second. She now had a duck in each hand held by the neck. They weren't heavy, but they were awkward, as she was wading through the water. Ian saw she had not found the second one and shouted.

"You're nearly on it. It's about ten yards to your left I think."

Then he shot his fourth duck which mercifully fell near to Katie, but as she turned she stumbled and fell flat in the water. Ian could not stop himself laughing. He just hoped she had not seen him. However she had! She did not let on, but got up and struggled until she had got all four ducks and made for the dry path. Ian knew better than to make any comment about the 'wet look', but thanked her for retrieving the ducks. He did make a mistake by saying,

"Well done. You are better than any Labrador." Katie just gave a rather false smile and said,

"Good shooting. You got four out of four."

As they walked back to the Landrover Ian told her about the species of duck which you found in Kenya. One of the ones he had shot had a white face. He said that was a 'White Faced Tree Duck'. He didn't really get the joke when Katie said,

"Are you sure you shot it. Perhaps it died of fright and that's why it's got a white face!"

It was not cold. Walking in totally soaked clothes was not much fun, but Katie did not complain. She trudged behind him on the narrow dry paths.

Luckily the 'Isaac Walton' had plenty of hot water. Katie washed out the mud from her clothes and 'tackies' and then had a lovely long shower. Ian had taken the ducks to the chef and organised their cooking. He met a couple who he knew from Nairobi so he invited them to join him and Katie for supper. He had a quick 'Tusker' with them before joining Katie who was happily drying her hair, having found a hair drier in a cupboard. Katie made a special effort now that she was clean. She looked lovely and Ian complimented her. She said as she did a little curtesy,

"Thank you kind Sir, I'm ready for a drink." So they walked arm in arm down the wide staircase to the restaurant. Ian introduced Katie to Paul and Janice. Katie was slightly surprised, but thought, now that she knew him so well, how typical it was of Ian. Actually she like surprises and she had really enjoyed their working trip so far. However she was determined to tease him in bed that night.

It appeared that Paul did not play rugby, but played hockey for Nairobi Club. Ian had met him as Ian played hockey when it wasn't the rugby season. Janice also played hockey for the ladies team. She turned to Katie,

"You ought to join us. It is good fun." Katie replied,

"I'd love to, but BOAC are not very accommodating. I never really know when I'm going to be in Kenya. Once I was only at Embakasi for twenty minutes. Ian met me. We only had time for a shag in the back of his Landrover and I had to rush back." She laughed and continued,

"It was great fun and well worth it!"

Paul who worked for 'Shell' looked horrified. Janice had a rather wistful look. Katie guessed she wouldn't mind a quick shag with Ian!

Anyhow because Janice was good fun, the evening went well. Ian, if he had not had several 'Tuskers' might have guessed that he was going to be teased later, as Katie gave a graphic demonstration of him treating her like a Labrador. She even added some arm waving and some 'go lefts' and 'high losts' for good measure. Then she described how she had gone face down in the water and that he had laughed, but had hoped she hadn't seen him laugh. Janice was in stitches with laughter. Paul was much more serious and was worried that Katie might have caught Bilharziasis. They went to bed saying they hoped they would meet for breakfast in the morning.

Katie was ready for bed first and jumped in to the deep feather mattress while Ian was in the bathroom. She was naked but took a belt into bed with her and quickly tied it tightly round her thighs above her knees by winding it around twice. She was sitting up with the sheets up under her breasts looking very sexy when Ian came in.

"I expect my ace water-fowler is too weary after his hard work shooting to satisfy his loyal picker-upper tonight?"

"I think I might be able to show my gratitude."

"Oh good, can you cuddle my back?"

This was not quite what he had in mind, but he had high hopes of softening her up. She switched off the lights and rolled over away from him, as she normally did if they were going to sleep cuddled together. Ian kissed her neck which he knew she loved and equally she knew was asking for sex. She wriggled her bottom invitingly and drew his top hand on to her breast. She felt him hard behind her, but as her thighs were tightly together he had to stay there slightly frustrated. He kissed her neck some more, fondled her breasts, brought his hand down and started to rub her. She arched her back. Then he sucked her ear lobes. She knew he was getting excited. So was she, but she was determined to tease him.

"High-lost, you will have to find it?"

Ian tried, but her thighs were tightly together. He started to tickle her which he knew would make her relax her thighs. She giggled, but her thighs stayed tightly together. He rubbed her harder. She started to pant and her tummy muscles tightened. He knew she must be very excited now and would let him into her. She gasped,

"What's happened to your '*mkia'?* I'm getting so ready for him!"

Still she would not part her thighs. He entered her with two fingers and felt her wetness. Then she sighed,

"Oh you found it. That was lovely. Sleep well my Darling."

She pretended to go to sleep. He kept kissing her neck. She loved it, as she knew he was getting frantic. He tried to part her legs with one of his legs and then he felt the belt.

"You are a little minx!" Katie giggled as she unclasped the belt,

"Just go a little bit left. You should be right on it now."

She rolled on to her tummy and pushed her bottom up into the air. He was on top of her in a second, but he remembered her tease and he entered her properly with two fingers and rhythmically went in and out quickly. Katie really came then. She grasped the sheets and bit the pillow and then she felt him fill her and she came again with him.

Eventually they both calmed down and Ian rolled off her on to his back and she moved across into his arms. She whispered,

"I love you, but you are an old bugger you know!"

"I love you so much. I don't know why you put up with me?"

They kissed and slept until dawn. She was still on top of him and she kissed him and then said,

"We must stink of sex. I'm hungry. Let's have quick showers and we can get down to breakfast?"

Paul and Janice, when they came into the dining room, were surprised that Katie and Ian had nearly finished theirs. Just to stir Paul up, Katie said,

"Sex always makes us hungry!"

Paul looking embarrassed and Janice sniggered. Katie and Ian said their goodbyes and left them eating their breakfast. Ian had to get to his office in Kabete in the afternoon and Katie was going to lie in the sun after lunch. She was pleased, as she still had another week left of her leave.

Nelson made them a good supper and Ian produced a bottle of red wine to go with the steaks. They actually were both quite tired and they were early to bed and had a good nights sleep.

They had a lovely lie-in. Nelson had left early so Ian made the tea. When he got back into bed, Katie said,

"As your personal rugby trainer, I'm afraid there is no sex for you this morning before the big game this afternoon. However I always find sex makes me a more energetic supporter so ……?" Ian replied,

"As I hope you will be wearing a short skirt and I haven't shaved, I don't want to embarrass you by giving you a rash on those lovely soft thighs!"

Katie smiled sweetly and slipped out of bed and went into the bathroom. Ian thought she was going for a wee. She came back with a mug of hot water, his shaving brush, a shaving stick and his safety razor. She made him sit up. She sat on thighs and very gently and carefully shaved his face. Ian could not hide the fact that he found it very erotic. Just before she got off the bed she rubbed herself on him which made him gasp with pleasure. She then washed off the soap with a flannel and dried his face with a towel. All the time her soft breasts brushed against him. Then her hand just happened to rest on his shaft and stroke it gently. As soon as she was back on the bed, Ian came down on her. Katie loved it and begged him not to stop until she was totally exhausted. He then moved up her body and started kissing her lips. Then when he was poised above her she giggled and said,

"Remember no sex before the big game." She could feel his excitement and wondered if he could resist her. He couldn't and with a deep sigh he entered her and came deep inside her. She clutched him to her, both with her legs and arms and said,

"That was lovely. I'm sure it is total bull shit about sex wearing you out before a big rugby game. I'm sure if we had been at it like rabbits all through the night it might affect your performance on the pitch but we've had a wonderful nights sleep. Good luck this afternoon. I will be cheering for you, you lovely man."

Katie enjoyed going to watch rugby. She met up with Jean and twins. The twins insisted that Katie kicked a ball with them. Jean tried to dissuade them, but Katie didn't mind. Katie surprised herself because she seemed to get on well with youngsters. The sun was shining, the ball was dry and clean. Soon she was teaching them how to catch a ball and how to dribble using her legs to keep the ball in a straight line. She was wearing quite a short skirt but it was khaki and so was her shirt so she demonstrated to the boys falling on the ball making sure their bodies were towards the attackers so that as the scrum formed the ball could be healed to their scrum half. Other young boys joined them and so they had enough to play five-a-side. She got one side to take off their shirts so they could play 'shirts and no shirts'. It was only when a man shouted out.

"Shouldn't you take off your shirt?" That Katie realised that there were several male spectators watching her, because she was showing rather a large amount of brown thigh when she was running. She was saved further embarrassment as she saw the players come on to the pitch and she could end her impromptu training session. She went back to Jean saying,

“Bloody hell, I'm sorry. I made a real spectacle of myself. I'm such a fool.” Jean smiled at her,

“I think you are marvellous and so do the twins. If I had great legs like you have got, I wouldn't mind showing them off.” Katie answered,

“I'm just worried that I will let Ian down and he will be teased.” Jean replied,

“You mustn't worry about that. Ian is a changed man. He used to be a real piss-head except when he was flying, now he is great fun at a party. He does not drink half as much. My husband says he is playing much better rugby.” Katie replied,

“I'm getting very fond of him, but it worries me that he is so much older than me.” Jean asked,

“How old are you. I know he is thirty so he can't be that much older than you.” Katie answered,

“I'm only eighteen.” Jean’s eyebrows shot up with surprise.

“Katie, you are quite amazing. I could no more get ten little boys to play a game of rugby than fly around the moon. You have certainly no need to worry about any age gap.”

Katie was delighted. She was so pleased that she had perhaps changed Ian’s life for the better. She supported ‘Nondes’ with even more gusto. Both Katie and Jean we're delighted that ‘Nondes’ had a good win. After the game and they had both got drinks, Jean said,

“Would you and Ian like to come to ours for a Bar-B-Q at lunch time tomorrow, or have you got to go off flying.” Katie answered,

“We'd love to. It is lovely I have got another week off.”

Jean smiled and thought, ‘*This girl is the one for Ian. She is just what he needs. It is interesting that she makes the plans for the two of them. Most girlfriends and even wives would ask their husbands.*’

Jean’s husband, John, joined them. When Jean said that she had invited Ian and Katie for lunch, John seemed delighted. Then Jean said,

“I'd better get the boys and take them home.” She disappeared into the throng of drinkers. John obviously found Katie attractive, but was tongue-tied. Katie to put him at his ease started talking about the rugby game. John then waxed eloquent about how well Ian had played. Katie was feeling in a devilish mood after the drink and said,

“So you you think I should give him a reward in bed tonight?” John spluttered something totally unintelligible, as Jean came up with the twins saying,

“Say goodnight to Daddy and goodbye to Katie. Are you pleased she and and Ian are coming to lunch tomorrow?”

“Yeah,” was their reply. Katie went down so they could both give her a hug. Jean mused to herself, ‘*It would appear that Katie is a hit with all the important men in my life.*’

Ian joined them. Katie gave him a big hug and said,

“Well done you were a star. John was just saying that I should give you a night to remember as you played so well. I hope you don't mind, but I have accepted Jean’s invitation to a Bar-B-Q tomorrow lunch time. Will we be able to get up to Molo OK in the dark?”

“Certainly that won't be a problem. You will be able to have a sleep on the way. It is a lovely old fashioned hotel. We will have a fire in our room. I will be able to give you a night to remember.” Katie gave him another hug and the way she held her body so close to his, did not go unnoticed by Jean who thought, ‘*I have got a lot to learn from this girl. She obviously enjoys sex and has taught Ian a thing or two. In the past I can imagine him just having a few drinks or may be several drinks and going to bed on his own. I'm going to wake John up. We treat sex as a twice weekly chore!*’

Jean said,

“Come on boys we must go home. It's time for a bath and then bed. You need to be up early tomorrow it's Sunday and you've got mini-rugby. You love that.” Derek said,

“I wish Katie was coming home to bath us,” Robert added,

“Katie, would you read us a storey?” Katie replied,

“No I won't read you a story,” Their faces fell, she continued, “but if you are really quick in the bath I will tell you a story. It is really blood-thirsty so I shouldn't think you would enjoy it.” They chorused, “Yes we would.”

So Katie came home with Jean and the twins. As they came into the house, Katie said,

“Into the bath, quick sharp,” The boys rushed off and Katie turned to Jean, “Have some time on your own. I imagine you don't get much?” Jean answered,

“Too right, I was only thinking when I saw you hugging Ian that I need to pep John up. I'm going to really tart myself up tonight. I hope he notices. However I expect he will have two many beers and be totally useless.” Katie laughed,

“Even if he has ‘Brewers Droop’ he can still make it good for you.”

“I hadn't thought of that. Look out John, there's going to be a sex bomb in your bed tonight!”

Jean was still putting on her make up, when she heard Katie talking quietly to their cook in Swahili. However had she managed to get the twins off to sleep so quickly?

When they were in the car, Katie said,

“Jean you look great.”

“Thanks Katie, I needed a confidence booster. I think this skirt is too short.”

“Rubbish, you've got great legs. I find just by showing my knickers, even if no one is looking gives me confidence.” Jean really laughed then,

“Katie you are impossible. I hope you didn't show my boys your knickers?”

“Of course not, but I told them a very lurid story about crusaders and saracens which seemed to send them to sleep!” Jean commented,

“I'm going to enjoy tonight! You must be seriously scary to frighten those two to sleep.”

“I did cheat. I did give them big hugs.”

“I will have to watch you Katie, giving my menfolk big hugs! Although I don't think John would even notice a big hug.”

“You might be favourably surprised Jean!”

“Let's hope so.”

Actually the two of them were noticed by several men, as they walked across from Parklands to ‘Nondes’. When they found John and Ian, Ian immediately bought them G & Ts. John said,

“That skirt’s a bit short!” Before Jean could say anything Katie started to tell him how her skirt had ridden up when she had driven Ian up to the NFD, when they had first met. She then, before Jean could stop her, lifted Jean’s skirt up to demonstrate where his rough face had given her a rash. John started to bluster,

"I would never do anything like that." Katie snorted, and then giggled,

"I bet you'd like to!"

John was lost for words. Two men who played for 'Nondes' who had noticed Katie and Jean coming over the grass had come over. Katie said,

"Hiya, I'm Katie and I'm sure you've know Jean. John and I are having a disagreement. I'm sure you guys are really honest and not shy. Can you help us decide whether John or I are correct?" The older, called Ken said,

"We can certainly try."

"Right," Said Katie. "You've got to be really honest and answer, yes or no. When you saw us walking over the grass in shorts skirts did you think? That's a great sight I can almost see their knickers."

Ken and Alister looked at each other and laughed. Then Ken said,

"I can't deny it. I said, wow, and Alister said, this is looking like a good party." Katie turned to John with a smirk saying,

"My case rests! So John would you like to retract your statement about the length of Jean's skirt and say something like, I like that skirt Jean, it shows off your lovely legs."

John puts his arms around Jean and said,

"I'm sorry I was such a miserable old sod. You have got great legs." Jean kissed him on the lips and hugged him. Ken and Alistair cheered. From then on it was a really good party. There was a lot of laughter and merriment.

In fact as the fun had started quite early, Katie and Ian got home in good time. As she got out of the Landrover, Ian swept her off her feet and carried her over the threshold saying,

"I want this to be a significant home coming. Thank you for last week it has been really good fun." As he put her down in the bedroom they kissed passionately. He pulled her to him and she could feel his excitement. As they parted, Katie said,

"I noticed you weren't drinking much like you do when you are flying in the morning. How about claiming your reward for playing so well?"

He nuzzled her neck and said,

"Just taking your clothes off and seeing you naked will be a wonderful reward." He got another passionate kiss and he felt her hand on his zip. Then she surprised him by saying rather breathlessly,

"You know how you only have to tickle me and somehow my legs fall apart and I let you do whatever you like which I really enjoy. However would you let me tie you up and so I could really tease you?"

"Sounds fun let's go for it."

Katie started undressing him with one hand and playing with him, with her other hand. Ian loved it and kept kissing her. She pushed him on to the bed and grabbed a handful of his silk ties which he so very rarely wore. She tied his arms and legs to the bed not very tightly but definitely securely. Still fully clothed she found one of her BOAC cravats and blind -folded him. Then she said

"We are gong to have a lovely game. When you get one of my questions right you are going to get a kiss or perhaps something more. I love you so much so we won't have any forfeits. I know I should play hard to get, but I can't pretend anything to you. I love you to bits." She kissed him again. Their tongues met. He sucked her bottom lip. She wanted him then so much she nearly stripped off and rode him, but she just managed to restrain herself. She got off the bed and stood up in front of him.

"Listen carefully," She took off her skirt.

"What piece of clothing have I taken off?"

"You've taken off your skirt."

"You're right." She got on the bed and kissed him and held his shaft gently in her hand. He groaned with pleasure. She moved down his body.

"I'm holding you and gently rubbing you on which part of me?"

"You are rubbing me on your thigh."

"Correct. Would you like to be more accurate?"

"You're rubbing me on the top of your thigh just inside your silk French knickers."

"Very good, would you like a little prize?" Ian answered,

"Oh please, that feels so good." Katie pushed him up the leg of her knickers and rubbed him with the silk. At the same time she kissed him. In her hand she could feel a throbbing. She stopped rubbing and broke from the kiss. He gasped,

"That was so lovely I nearly came."

“I know I felt you throbbing. We will slow down a little. She got off him and took off her knickers.

“What did I take off?”

“You took off your knickers. There was a little crackle of static from your pubic hair! Christ. I want you. This is unbearable.” She giggled,

“It's meant to be. I can assure you it is very exciting for me. Feel me.” She brought herself over his hand so he could feel how wet she was.

Then she took off her blouse. “Have I taken off my bra?”

“No that was only your blouse.”

“Would you like to take off my bra?”

“Oh yes. I so want to suck your nipples.”

“You have been very good so far so I will allow that.”

She lay on her back on top of him so Ian could unclip her bra with his teeth. Then she rolled over and she brought her tits and held them to his mouth. He sucked greedily. She started to pant and then sighed,

“You know you just gave me an orgasm. Now I am so fired up I don't think I can play anymore. I so want you. She started rubbing herself on his thigh. He whispered in her ear.

“Keep rubbing. Come for me my darling.”

Then she came and he could actually feel her stickiness on his thigh. He said,

“You are a lovely sexy girl. That was such a wonderful reward.” In her ecstasy she did not forget that he had yet to have an orgasm. What a wonderful, kind man he was.

When she was a bit calmer she said,

“I so want to tease you and make it ecstatic for you. What part of me is touching your manhood now?” She was softly licking him.

“Your tongue is licking me. It's lovely.” She stopped and took his tip to her ear.

“What is he touching now?”

He sighed,

“I'm not sure, your ear?”

“That is correct and now?”

“I’m touching your nipple.”

“Correct. Will you come if I gently rub you?”

"Yes, Oh yes. I'm trying not to, but oh it is too much." His hot semen came on her breasts. She took some to her mouth with her fingers and sucked them. Then she moved up him so he could lick her breasts. It was lovely. His tongue was so gentle then he started sucking again. Her groin was aching. She brought her thighs up beside his head and he licked her delicate lips. He licked inside her lips. He licked her tiny nob. It was wonderful. He then started licking her harder and harder until she came. She cried out and came again and still he licked. It was too much, but she still could not stop herself rocking rhythmically on his tongue. He felt her thighs squeeze his face. Then she moved down his body. She was so moist that he did not even know he was inside her, until he felt her gripping him with her vagina. He came deep inside her. She flopped forward and their mouths locked. They held their breaths and then they gasped, as if they were drowning. Katie was not sure if she had lost consciousness for a second. Then she felt him sucking her ear-loop. She just lay there breathing in. She was not sure how she untied him, but it was dawn when she woke to feel his strong arms around her. She felt so loved and cherished. He realised she had woken and whispered,

"I love you so much. It is not just the sex. It is your wonderful sense of adventure and fun. They kissed deeply. Katie then whispered,

"I was meant to be giving you a reward and you gave me the most wonderful time of my life. Can you enter me again?"

She felt him, as she rolled on to her back and drew her feet up so she was a wide open as she could be. Then they trust together. She laughed happily,

"You are obviously not worried that a lion is going to eat you. You are taking a lovely long time. I'm getting there. Yes I'm nearly there." He gripped her small bottom in his big strong hands to try to stop himself, until he felt her hot mouth on his neck. She did not bite but sucked his skin. He came crying,

"Katie, Katie, my darling."

They lay together until the sun's rays were pouring through the windows. Katie giggled,

"We're naughty children. We did not even draw the curtains!" Ian added,

“I don't think I even locked the door. I'm sure a thief could have totally cleaned out the house and I wouldn't have heard a thing. Your lovemaking was so magical. Now you lie and snooze. I will make some tea and run you a bath.”

She reached up and kissed him on the lips.

“That will be great, but please join me in the bath. I would love you to wash my hair.”

It was past ten before they sat on the veranda to have breakfast. When they had finished and Ian pushed the low chair away from the table, she came and sat in his lap. She kissed him softly saying,

“You are amazing. I can still feel you hard. It's just a pity your manhood is not a bit bigger!” He kept tickling her until she begged him to stop.

When Katie drove the Landrover into John and Jean’s drive, the twins rushed out to greet them. They then heard all about the mini-rugby. Katie could see, as soon as she came into the kitchen that Jean was on top form. She had shorts on and was wearing an apron which looked very sexy not only from the back, as it showed off her pert bottom, but also from the from the front as it was not obvious she had anything underneath it. Katie whispered,

“Did you have fun?” Jean replied,

“And how. It was great. Oh thank you Katie.” No more was said but they all had a good lunch.

Chapter 8

The second week is just as much fun

Katie was grateful to Ian as she could see he was holding back on the beers. As soon as they had said their goodbyes and were on the road, Ian said,

"You make yourself comfortable and have a good sleep. I threw in several pillows they are just behind you. As she leant over she felt his hand up her skirt between her legs. She turned and kissed his neck,

"You rascal, but I love it." As she made herself comfortable with her head in his groin his shorts rode up and she licked the tip of his Willy.

"Who is the rascal now? But like you I love it."

She pulled his shorts down and after nuzzling him she was soon asleep. He managed to keep driving but only just. Her brown thighs were so tempting. She slept the whole way to Molo and only woke when he turned off the Landrover. She pushed herself up. Gave him a quick kiss and said,

"That was a marvellous sleep. I went to sleep dreaming of our lovemaking and here we are. You are right about this place being cool. I'm bloody freezing. I almost wish I had stockings on. I would then look a right trollop in this short skirt. They grabbed their small bags and were soon in the warm bar. They then had a bowl of hot soup and a sherry each and then they went to their room. The fire was blazing merrily. Katie jumped and bounced on the bed saying,

"This really won't do, we haven't made love for over twelve hours!" Ian turned after he had unpacked his bag to find Katie on her knees naked on the sheep skin rug on the floor looking up at him smiling. He turned off the lights, so she was just lit by the firelight. He took off his clothes as rapidly as he could and came up behind her. She fell on to her elbows and wiggled her bottom enticingly. He reached between her legs and gently rubbed her, as he kissed the back of her neck. She arched her back and pushed back on to his hand, as he entered her with his fingers. He watched with delight as the fire light lit her lovely body undulating in time with his hand. It was only after he had seen her bury her face in the rug that he entered her from behind, putting his hands around her and fondling her breasts. He was so excited, he just had to thrust twice and then he pushed deep into her with a satisfied sigh.

Even with the fire it was not that warm and they were soon in bed. Ian thought they would soon be asleep and he cuddled up behind her. He had forgotten that she had been sleeping all the way up to Molo and that he had promised her another night of excitement. He felt a little hand holding him, as she pushed him on to his back. She burrowed down the bed and took him in her mouth and then did wicked things to him. It was not long before he came into her mouth. She then wriggled up the bed and kissed him passionately. The taste in her mouth excited him. He reached down between her legs and rubbed her vigorously as they continued to kiss. Then she sat up wrapping the bed clothes around her. She pushed him inside her and then she rode him. He helped her with his hands on her bottom. It was several minutes before he came this time and then she collapsed on top of him and was soon asleep.

They were up in good time in the morning to a massive breakfast. Katie set off driving. Ian said,

"I'm a little tired. I think I'll have a little sleep?" This was greeted with,

"I know you shaved this morning but you can dream on if you think that cheeky face of yours is coming anywhere near my groin. This is quite a busy road. I can imagine the ribald comments in 'Nondes' if I'm caught with your head in my lap. I have got such a bad reputation now, that everyone will know I encouraged you! I expected a comment about these knickers which I got in London, but I think you are bored with me now and you don't bother to have a peep when I get into the Landrover." She tried to stop him but she was too slow. He flipped up her skirt, saying,

"Yes, they get my full approval, as do the lovely thighs below them."

"You are full of bull this morning." Secretly she was delighted with the comment and the feather like stroke she got with his right hand.

They journeyed on gaining altitude towards Kericho. Katie was fascinated by the vast acreage of bright green tea bushes. She could see the ladies with their large baskets picking the small tea shoots which would eventually be processed into packets to make some of the finest tea in the world. Ian explained about the weather. Every morning the sun would come up and there would not be a cloud in the sky. Then slowly the cloud would build up, as it was now, towards 4 o'clock and then it would rain. This would then clear in the late evening. The regular rain accounted for the high rainfall which tea growing required. The altitude was an added bonus, as it meant Kericho was a lovely cool place but had plenty of sun.

They made their way to the veterinary office. Ian discussed the problem of the holding ground in Sotik with Elliott, the DVO, while the staff made Katie a cup of tea. Ian said he would visit it later in the week.

Elliott said that he was delighted that Ian had come that day, as there was going to be a clay pigeon shoot this evening when the rain had finished. There was a match between the 'tea guys' and the 'civil servants'. Elliott asked if Ian would be in the 'civil servants' team. He said they would still be one short. Katie said,

"I have done a little clay pigeon shooting. I could join the team, if you could put up with me. I'm afraid I'm not much good but I could put on a short skirt which might put the old 'tea guys' off!" Elliott liked the idea of the short skirt. Ian said,

"You never did any duck shooting. I'm sorry I never realised you could shoot." Katie replied,

"As I said, I'm rather soft hearted and felt sorry for the ducks. I'm not bothered about the clays!" Then she told Elliott about Ian treating her like a gun-dog and her falling flat on her face in the rice paddy. Elliott thought that was amusing, when she added that she had kept her thighs tightly together that night to punish Ian he thought it was hilarious.

They left Elliott and made their way to the 'Kericho Tea Hotel'. He said he would see them latter as the match was going to be at the hotel.

Katie was enchanted by the large old fashioned hotel. She loved the enormous bath which stood in the middle of the bathroom. She decided to have a bath and a hair wash as the journey had been dusty. She persuaded Ian to join her. He didn't need much persuading. Katie was also pleased, as there was a large fan which acted like a hair dryer. Ian caught her standing in front of it in the nude with her legs wide apart and lovely blond hair streaming out behind her. She giggled and said it was rather an erotic experience. When Ian suggested they had time for a quick cuddle, Katie demurred saying sex might put her off her shooting! She said they would have great fun later on, as she saw there was a fire in their room. Ian remembered the fire and sheep skin rug at Molo, so he was very happy to wait.

He noticed she wore a very short skirt. In fact it was so short that he claimed he could actually see her knickers if she just bent over, let alone if she had to get up into a Landrover. Katie said she wasn't worried, as the match was at the hotel, so what anyone could see when she got into a Landrover was not relevant. Then to Ian's delight she proceeded to bend over with her back to the full length mirror to see what anyone could see. Then she decided the skirt was a little too short, but she made no effort to change it, but gave him a demonstration of her picking things up off the floor in a very genteel manner with her legs tightly together and bending her knees. In fact Ian found that even sexier, as it made him use his imagination.

They went down to the foyer of the hotel. Obviously the 'tea guys' knocked off early in the afternoon as they were all in the bar, when Ian and Katie walked in. They could not keep their eyes off Katie and had no idea that she and Ian were anything to do with the clay pigeon shoot. There were teams of four. Elliott arrived with Gordon, the government doctor who made up the final member of their team. He was a young bachelor and also was very impressed with Katie. Katie smiled to herself, as she imagined him being very shy and embarrassed if she had come into his consulting room. The four 'tea guys' came over. Their captain, Reginald said to Elliott,

"Pity you couldn't find a fourth." He turned to Ian and said,

"So you are new to the district?" Ian replied,

"No, I'm a visitor from Kabete." Elliott added,

"I hope you don't mind if Katie is in our team. She is an air hostess so actually she isn't a civil servant." Reginald's eyes travelled up Katie's legs, lingered at the bottom of her skirt, went on up and really lingered on her chest. He managed a very affable,

"That will be fine. We have never had a young lady shooting before." Katie held out her hand and gave him a big smile,

"I'm Katie. You will have to make allowances for me as I haven't done very much. Perhaps you could help me with my swing?" Reginald's eyes lit up as he imagined putting his arms around her from behind and having a wonderful view of her cleavage. They walked out to the car park to get the guns. Elliott was happy for Ian to borrow his gun and Gordon was happy for Katie to have his. The 'tea guys' made a big fuss about getting their guns out of leather box type cases. Elliott and Gordon only had gun sleeves.

One of the 'tea guys' called, Archibald had a thick padded gilet with leather over the shoulders. Katie approached him fluttering her eye lashes and asked if she could borrow it, when she shot, so that she did not bruise her shoulder. He went to take it off, but Katie stopped him saying,

"It would be lovely if you can warm it up for me. It would then be all snugly and cuddly." Archibald went very red as he imagined being all snugly and cuddly with Katie.

There were two clay pigeon traps set up, one from each side. Another of the 'tea guys' called Percy made a fuss about getting the right tension on the spring. The operator had a little seat to sit on. After Percy had released the trap a couple of times, Katie lent down towards him saying,

"I expect you have to be ever so strong to work that?" He looked straight down her front and as Katie whispered to Ian later. She thought he probably could see her nipples. Percy said,

"It's not really strength but a knack actually. Do have a go. He got off the seat. Katie lifted a long elegant leg a little higher than was necessary and sat down on the seat. She whispered to Percy with a giggle,

"I will have to be very careful sitting on this or you will be able to see my knickers. They are a little bit on the skimpy side." Percy went very red in the face and his glasses misted up. Reginald did not want to miss out on the action. He asked Katie,

“Would you like to have a couple of practice swings with me to help you?” Katie replied,

“That would be super.”

Archibald made a big song and dance of getting out of his gilet. Katie gave a little shiver as she put it on which made her breasts giggle delightfully. It was much too big for her so it was lower enough not to hide her chest but she made sure the padding was just in the right place on her shoulder. So Percy released a couple of clays as Reginald put his arms around her. She missed them both. Percy said,

“Have one more for luck.” Katie missed it as well but followed through and hit a real Green Pigeon which was coming home to roost. In fact this was really bad form, but because Katie was such an attraction, there was a lot of guffawing. Katie insisted on retrieving it and hugging it to her breast. All the ‘tea guys’ insisted on examining it.

So they started the competition. There was no doubt that the ‘tea guys’ were better and more practiced shots. However they seemed to have certain deficiencies when Katie bent down to pick daisies to make a daisy chain. Perry always missed the first two of his shots when Katie insisted on working the trap. Ian thought it was hilarious that somehow she could not manage to sit on the seat without showing virtually all of her knickers. Equally she always seemed to manage to lean forward just before one of the ‘tea guys’ was about to shoot. Also it was strange that at the very start, Katie had missed all three of the clays and yet when she was shooting later she seemed to be the best of her team.

The final session was two clays, on from each side, which was then repeated. The gun said pull and shot at the first clay the second clay was launched when the trap operator heard the first shot. The ‘tea guys’ had won unless Katie who was the final gun hit all four clays. She smoothly did it, so that it was a draw. Elliott and Gordon were delighted. The ‘tea guys’ did not appear to realise that they had been hustled. They insisted on buying the drinks. They all sat down to a shoot supper which everyone seemed to enjoy. Ian could not wait to get Katie up to their room. He came up behind her and pretended to teach her to swing the gun. He kissed her neck.

"You are a real little flirt. I can definitely see those lovely pink nipples." Katie retorted,

"Well you didn't want to lose did you?" Ian laughed and said,

"Please pretend to sit down on the trap seat." Katie gave a very good demonstration. Ian whistled. "I definitely could see your bush. You are so bloody sexy." She answered,

"I'm glad you think so."

The rest of the week in theory Ian worked hard. He had to find sites for single-man government veterinary practices in Nyanza and Western Provinces. Katie did most of the driving which she enjoyed. They had to visit Kisi, Kisumu and Maseno in Nyanza Province. They stayed in Maseno with Alan Howkins who had played Rugby against Ian. He was delighted to meet Katie and said,

"Next time when we have to have a visit from head office, you just come on your own Katie. I'm sure you and I can work something out. You can leave Ian to pounce about in his big important office in Kabete." Katie gave him a big smile and replied,

"It depends on quite what we have to work out!"

The next morning they did some skiving. They crossed over into Uganda illegally and went white water rafting on the Nile. Somehow Katie had managed to lose her bikini somewhere in the Landrover. Ian was delighted and said she would look really sexy in a top and her shorts. In reality they had to wear wet suits. Katie therefore kept her shorts and top dry and was naked in the wet suit. Ian spent most of the morning trying to pull down the zip which went from her neck to her crutch, without her knowing. Initially Katie kept pulling it back up, then she decided to call his bluff and just left it unzipped! Ian was then forced to pull it back up, saying,

"I can't have my driver wandering about with her tits hanging out!"

The white water rafting was not very severe, but they had a good laugh. They were the only guys doing it, so they had a fun time with the gap year student who was meant to be their instructor. He didn't realise that Katie had nothing on under her wet suit until the end. She thought he would probably have capsized them on purpose if he had known earlier.

They made their way into Western Province once again crossing the border on Mount Elgon illegally. There were said to be gorillas in the area, but they didn't see any evidence.

Ian told Katie about a famous Hollywood movie which was meant to be set in Africa, but actually was filmed totally on set in Hollywood. Clarke Gabriel had a very manly line to the heroine, 'There are gorillas in those hills!' Katie said,

"I remember my mother fancied Clarke Gabriel. Therefore I do remember what he looked like. He was rather dishy. I suppose I could dream of him tonight while you are snoring behind me. What a poor girl has to put up with!"

The efficient DVO at Busia, Tony Tomkins had already found a good site so they had a quick cup of coffee wth him. Ian made extensive notes. Tony seemed very happy to chat to Katie. When they arrived at Bungoma, although the veterinary office was fully manned with lay staff, the DVO who was a keen ornithologist was AWOL. Ian whispered to Katie,

"After what we have been up to this morning, I think we will keep quiet about this. What happens in Bungoma stays in Bungoma." Katie added with a very serious face,

"I agree. If your driver has her tits hanging out when rafting on the Nile, it is 'What happens on the Nile stays on the Nile.' We will have no more chauvinistic remarks from you young man!" Ian murmured,

"I'm sorry." She laughed,

"I was only pulling your leg. You are so easy to tease. Come on let's find a site for this vet practice and we can go and find a sitatunga."

The head veterinary scout had some ideas for sites, so with Katie driving and Ian siting in the middle seat with his right hand on her thigh, he claimed there was nowhere else to put it, they set off around the town. Ian made notes about the four possible sites and having dropped the helpful veterinary scout back at the office, they made their way to Kakamega Forest which Ian thought was the only place you could find sitatunga in Kenya.

A sitatunga is a small antelope which likes to live in swamps. It is the only antelope which has become totally adapted to an aquatic environment. It has long splayed out hoofs, which allows it to move very swiftly in mud. It can swim and stay hidden under water with just the tip of its nose above the surface.

Ever cheerful Katie said, as it began to rain,

"I'm sure this is just the weather to find an elusive sitatunga! However shall we scrub round camping and go and stay in a lovely hotel with a fire in our room?"

However Ian felt they ought to try. They failed. The rain continued. Supper was a disaster as Katie tried to cook a fry up in the dry in the back of the Landrover and got fat everywhere. Ian got soaked erecting the tent on the roof. However he did manage to keep the bedding dry. Katie got the tent organised and got into the double sleeping-bag while Ian did the washing up. Katie had some experience of his washing up and she knew that the next time she used the plates they would be smeared with fat. Katie had been quite cold when they arrived in the forest, so she had put on some stockings with a suspender belt under a pair of jeans. She got into the sleeping bag fully clothed. Ian clambered up the ladder in his water-proofs and was rather slow doing up the tent. Katie pretended to be cross,

"I bet Clarke Gabriel did not get the heroine soaking when he was protecting her from the gorillas. You had better take all that kit off or you will make the sleeping bag wet." Ian did as he was told. He only realised she was teasing, when he got into bed naked and shivering, only to find her fully clothed. He moaned and Katie said,

"Come on. Let me hug you. I will soon make you warm." He retorted,

"Bloody hell, you have so many clothes on. I won't feel any of your body heat!" Katie laughed at him,

"It seems only yesterday when I was a young virgin and you were so shy I had to ask you to undress me in bed. Where has the romance gone?"

Ian had got right into the sleeping bag and had zipped it up. He started to kiss her with some passion. He heard,

"That's better." Then he felt her hand and heard,

"Oh dear, I've been looking forward to this moment long and hard, but sadly you are neither." He growled,

"You are a little minx." Katie felt him fumbling with the top button of her jeans. She knew any moment he would pull the button off, so she helped him. Even with her help, Ian struggled to get her jeans off. However the exertion and the excitement started to warm him up. Katie said,

“I definitely feel a vast improvement!” She had purposely put her suspender belt and stockings over her knickers to make life harder for him. It slightly worried her that she found his fumbling so exciting. She knew he found it exciting, as he was breathing harder. She asked him,

“Am I abnormal finding it sexy with you trying to get my underwear off?” This straight forward question stopped him in his tracks. His heart and respiratory rate decreased while he was thinking up the answer. Katie was surprised. She thought, ‘*Men are strange, or perhaps it is this man. He was frantic to have sex a second ago. Now that he is thinking, he has calmed down.*’ Ian answered,

“I wish I understood. I only have experience with you.” Katie was still laughing,

“Come on Ian, you are thirty. I believed you when you said you were a virgin but I don't believe that you have never had any fumbling in the dark with a girl.”

“Certainly I have, but she has never told me what she liked or wanted. I've had to guess and hope she is enjoying it.” Katie kissed him and then said,

“Well you have guessed right most of the time with me. Do you mind if I help you?”

“No, I don't mind. I would love that.”

“Great. Lesson number one, as I know I have told you when we have been talking about cows, is that most of the time you need to go slowly. I know occasionally that I want you desperately, but those times will be pretty obvious.” Then she giggled,

“I can't afford to let you rip all my expensive knickers!”

Ian had not waited for anymore lessons and had put his hand in the front of her knickers. Katie said,

“I don't remember telling you to do that, but it is lovely.”

Slowly her clothes came off. She rolled on to her back and he had entered her. In a husky voice she said, as she wrapped her legs over his back and thrust her pelvis up to meet him,

“I might be dreaming of England but what is in my mind is the thought of your hard cock rubbing me.” She stopped talking and kissed him passionately. Ian's hands were on her bottom. He pushed her thighs down and rolled her on top of him. She rode him until they both gasped together. She flopped on him, his arms came around her and they slept as the heavy rain drummed on the tent. Soon Katie whispered, as they moved into their normal sleeping position,

"You're a star pupil."

She wasn't sure if he was actually asleep or awake but he gently fondled her breasts and she was sure then that he had dropped off. She did not remember anything more until morning.

The sun came up. The sky was a brilliant blue and the temperature rose which was lucky as they both had to come out of the tent and down the ladder for a wee. Ian volunteered for her to go back into the warm sleeping bag and he would make tea, however she quickly got into some clothes and helped him to sort out the Landrover. They had a Spartan breakfast of cereal, banana and UHT milk and were soon on the road.

They travelled on to Sotik where Ian had to inspect a LMD holding ground. There was nobody about when they got there, but they both could see the problem. The Israelis had made the new road right through the middle of the land. One side had a large stream running through it so any cattle that side had access to it for water. Now, because of the road, the other side had no water. Ian said,

"They are silly buggers. They will have to pipe water under the road. They will moan, as it will be costly and they have moved all their equipment away now. However the Israelis will do it OK." The sun was shining and so they sat and had a cup of coffee which they had made in one of Ian's thermoses, while they were packing up. Ian got out a rug for Katie to sit on saying,

"I would hate the new knickers and that pretty bottom to get damp." She replied,

"I know just what you are after young man, but the answer is definitely, no. I can easily imagine someone we know coming down the new road and seeing us having a romp on the grass. It isn't even very long!"

"I can assure you, no such naughty thoughts were on my mind."

She gave him a kiss, touched the front of his shorts and replied,

“You're a bloody liar, Richardson. When I'm next in London, I'm going to buy a chastity belt and keep it locked except on special occasions and ration you like these other girls at ‘Nondes’.

As they were walking back to the Landrover, holding hands, Ian said,

“You enjoy it too much!” She answered with a smile,

“I do occasionally, but normally I just lie on my back like a dutiful girlfriend and dream of England!”

Their destination was the Masai Mara Game Reserve, via Bommet. They bypassed the lodge at Governors Camp and made their way along the Mara River. They found a good camping spot with plenty of shade. It was not strictly allowed, but Ian was confident that they would not be discovered.

They had three blissful days out in the wilds. Katie had to wear her tackies because of the thorns but she did not bother with clothes. Ian was not so bold and wore a pair of shorts. Their camp was fairly primitive. They kept a crate of beer in the river so that the beers were cold. Ian would not let Katie go near the river, as he was frightened she would be taken by a croc. He rigged up an elaborate system for hauling water for washing out of the river with a bucket and some rope. Katie was sure the water was so dirty that she got dirtier each shower. However she found a shower very refreshing and she was sure the brown water helped her to tan. Because they kept a small fire going all the time with the big metal bucket, full of water beside it, they always had hot water. Katie found there was a definite improvement in Ian’s washing up!

They went for lovely walks into the bush. These were strictly illegal, but they were in such a remote part of the Masai Mara Game Reserve they thought they were pretty safe. They never saw any Game Department or Game Park vehicles. They were very nearly caught by a two Landrovers full of tourists. Katie who was totally nude, saw them first and shot behind a baobab tree dragging a less quick-witted Ian with her. She made Ian laugh by saying,

“I wish I had a brown paper bag to put over my head. I don't mind them seeing my body but it is being recognised by a senior BOAC captain that I want to avoid!”

The Landrovers came close enough to their hiding place that they could hear their voices. They were definitely speaking English. Katie said,

"I feel very wanton. How about it? I think it is the thought of being caught!"

They made love, standing up against the tree!

The time raced by. They totally cleared up the camp. No one would have known they had been there. Katie insisted on being naked for as long as possible and only put on her bikini top when they had been driving towards the entrance to the park and saw a mini bus coming towards them. As she was driving she had to lean forward and get Ian to tie it at the back. He asked,

"What about putting on the bottom half?"

"That's not required until we are in proper traffic."

"I will treasure the memory of this vision of you in my mind for the days ahead when you are away. Let's hope you get another stop over soon."

Chapter 9

A Flying safari to Alia Bay

It was 9.00am. Ian was now in a bit of a panic, driving back to his home. He had been to his office at the Veterinary Laboratories and had been working on a new wall map of the NFD which he was adapting, so that, not only could he see where the mobs LMD cattle were at any moment in time, but also, by means of coloured magnets, he could see their disease status. Then he had been summons by the Director of Veterinary Services (DVS) who was the God of Ian's world. Actually the DVS rated Ian very highly, but he never let on and always bollocked Ian for any misdemeanour to keep him in his place.

The DVS did not mince his words,

"I hear from a reliable source in Ethiopia that cattle are dying in large numbers by the Omo River. I want you to get up there, find out why they are dying, and report back to me yesterday. I don't want to know how you do it. I don't want any Kenyan staff involved until I know what the problem is, who owns the cattle and in which country they normally reside. If you are caught in Ethiopia, you are on your own. Do I make myself clearly understood?"

"You do Sir."

Ian did not like the sound of this assignment, particularly as he had to keep all his colleagues in the dark. He had told his PA that he was going to check on the health of some cattle in the NFD. This was so vague as to be laughable. His PA was a bright young Kikuyu guy who had delivered the summons and so knew that this was an assignment authorised by the DVS, but he knew nothing else. Ian had asked him to book a Cherokee Arrow, the fastest plane he was checked out on, for three days from the aero club, and to order some extra fuel in twenty five litre cans. Ian had then collected the stuff he was likely to need from the office, before rushing back to his home to get the kit he would need from there.

There was a taxi in the drive. He asked the driver in Swahili what he wanted. The driver said the Memsahib had told him to wait in case she wanted him to take her back into Nairobi. Ian was delighted. He was sure it must be Katie. He ran into the house. Katie was talking to Nelson. She turned and saw Ian. Then, much to Nelson's amusement, she wrapped her arms around Ian and kissed him passionately.

"I have so missed you. Sadly I have only two nights. I have to be at Embakasi by 7.30pm in three days time." Ian looked thoughtful.

"We could just make it, but our time is going to be short. Do you want to come on a two night really rough safari? I mean rough."

"What a thing to ask me. The only reason I went with you at all was because you offered me a really rough safari. Within five minutes that rough unshaven chin had given me a rash on my delicate thighs. What could be rougher than that?" Ian didn't reply, but gave Nelson twenty shillings and asked him to release the taxi driver.

Ian explained to a delighted Katie what they had to do. She realised that timing was going to be tight, so she packed her flight bag ready to go to work. She borrowed Ian's *kikapu (*a Kenyan woven basket) and put flight clothes and shoes ready for a quick change on their return. Ian shouted,

"Katie, it is not going to be like in the Landrover. We have to take extra fuel so weight of luggage must be minimal. It's going to be hot so you won't need pyjamas."

He came into the bedroom to find Katie in the nude. She turned, smiled and said,

"If I can borrow your tooth brush, I think these are all I need?" She held up a packet of her contraceptive pills. Then with a wicked grin she said,

"I could bring a pair of knickers for sleeping in if the pills are too heavy!" He gave her bottom a squeeze and said,

"I really don't know what I'm going to do with you!"

They drove to the aero club at break neck speed. Katie stroked his thigh,

"You know you have never flown me before. I'm really looking forward to it. Will you be all serious and very professional?"

He answered, “Yes, I think one has to be. If not I think it is rather easy to die.”

“I suppose you’re right. It's just that Jeanine is always boasting about being a member of the ‘Mile high club’ and I thought it would be fun to join” Ian laughed,

“Now that would be good fun!”

They took off with Ian encouraging Katie to hold the controls and use her feet on the pedals. Katie loved it and gave him a little kiss on his neck. Once they were on their heading to Alia Bay, Ian got her to keep the plane on that heading and slowly to keep climbing. He got his map out and a small note pad and started working out their fuel consumption. He was nervous that he had not brought enough extra cans. He felt Katie’s hand on his thigh which always excited him. He looked round. She was naked and looking at the altimeter. She said very seriously,

“Taking account of the fact that the ground is six thousand feet above sea level, I reckon we are a mile high. I am ready to join the club. Can you move your seat back as far as it will go and I will sit in your lap, after you have taken your shorts off?” Ian laughed,

“Whose is in charge of this plane?

“I am of course. You are just a vet. I am trained air crew! Get those shorts off. I've got myself excited just thinking about it.”

Once she was sitting in his lap, she wriggled her bottom provocatively and asked him to rub her while she kept the plane on the correct heading. She was really moving her bottom now and gave a big sigh.

“That was lovely. I'm a member now.” Then she gave a delightful little giggle.

“I think I will have a little sleep now. Can you manage?”

“No, I bloody well can't!”

She lent forward and directed him inside her. Then she teased,

“A modern girl has to do everything, fly the plane and pleasure the pilot.” She moved and Ian pushed upwards.

“Wow that feels rather good. In fact that feels extremely good.” Ian was gasping,

“Do you want to join the club now, my darling?”

She rhythmically moved her bottom. Ian shut his eyes, cupped her breasts and climaxed. Katie said,

"Bloody hell we are meant to be flying beside Lake Rudolf, now we are flying across it!"

She moved off his lap and on to her own seat. She turned and kissed his lips.

"Thank you that was great fun. Are we nearly there yet?"

They landed at Alia Bay in plenty of time with over an hour of daylight left to organise their camp. Compared to Ian's normal camp this was very substandard. He was thankful he had brought a tent as the wind got up. It was not cold but the dust would have been annoying. They were soon in it once they had made the preparations for an early start. Ian cuddled Katie's back until she whispered,

"I can feel him as hard as a stick. Aren't you a little frustrated?" Ian felt her move his hand lower. He felt the electric feel of her bush. She was just slightly damp.

"I thought as we had got to make an early start and we had made love in the plane that you would want to get to sleep." She sighed and replied,

"Well you thought wrong, but if you would rather get to sleep that's fine with me." Ian started kissing her tenderly on her neck and rubbing the tops of her thighs. She giggled,

"I think that means you would like a bit of hankie pankie. Well so would I." She sucked her fingers and as she felt him between her legs she started to rub him with her moist hand. He groaned with pleasure and put his fingers in his mouth and then with his wet fingers he rubbed the top of her nipple. Katie was in ecstasy. She did not need to suck her fingers she just rubbed him on her tender sensitive spot. Then she whispered,

"Can I come on top I so want to feel you deep inside me?" As she rolled on top of him and he entered her she added,

"See how ready I am. Oh that is so good with you holding my buttocks." Then they were kissing, sucking each other's tongue, sucking each other's bottom lips. All the time Ian was thrusting into her until she could bare it no longer. Their lips separated, she cried out and went weak, He gave one last thrust and she felt him fill her.

She was still on top of him when the alarm woke them. Katie gave him a little kiss.

"Sometimes, my love, you get it just right. Last night was one of those nights."

It was still dark. They didn't waste anytime, but quickly packed everything in the plane and locked it, although theft in this remote area was unlikely.

Ian had walked from this airstrip north before, to check on the most northern vaccination crush on the eastern side of Lake Rudolf. He had vaccinated cattle belonging to the Rendile tribe. They are in the same tribal group as the Masai and the Samburu. The DVS had been sparring with any information, as to whether Rendile cattle were dying. Ian guessed that the DVS did not know. The tip off had probably come from the OIE (World Organisation for Animal Health).

Initially they followed the road which really was little more than two parallel tracks with vegetation in the middle. Ian made Katie walk behind him, so she would be less likely to be scratched by the sharp thorns on the bushes. He was in a dilemma, as he wanted them to keep quiet, but he did not want to step on a snake. He thought snakes would be unlikely here but he had heard they were bad by the Omo River.

The quick African dawn came just before they reached the crush. From now on it was new territory for Ian. He knew Lake Rudolf was on his left and the Omo River Delta flowed into it only about a mile further north. All there was marking the border between Kenya and Ethiopia was a concrete round trig point. He planned just to keep heading north. There were no more twin tracks just a single path, so he followed it always checking his compass. He made a blaze on each tree he passed to help guide them back.

They smelt the dead cow before they saw it. It was really only a skeleton which had been picked clean by the vultures. Ian had no way of knowing the cause of death. They continued walking. Ian felt a sharp needle stab on his fore arm and then a slap from Katie in the same place. She pointed to a large dead fly on the ground. Ian whispered,

"Thanks that's a Tsetse fly. You have probably solved the riddle of the cattle deaths. As far as I'm aware, Tsetse flies are not found in this area normally. They spread three nasty Protozoan diseases which kill cattle." They continued and Ian was bitten twice more. Katie thought the flies were probably going for him, as he was leading. They were obviously in elephant country as they found the dung, but it was dry and so not recent. Then they started seeing cattle dung which was also dry. The path became more confusing. There were now several paths all mainly heading north. Ian took the left hand one, as he hoped to reach the river and get his bearings. There were more trees for him to blaze and the bush was thinner. Then they arrived on the bank of the river. It was muddy brown like the Ewaso Ng'iro but not as wide. Ian touched Katie's arm and pointed at the snout of a crocodile. Ian made several blazes on the trees so he would definitely recognise this spot on their return. Soon they came to a place where the bank was not so steep and it was obvious that cattle had been watered there recently.

They left the water and followed the cattle trails. Katie was following close behind him when a sudden movement of green caught his eye. He whirled round at head height and slashed with the panga. Katie leapt backwards. A green snake in a tree had struck at her. Ian had cut its head off which lay at her feet, together with its body which continued to writhe on the ground. She came into his arms. He stroked her hair,

"That was close. They are deadly. It was a green mamba. They tend to live in foliage."

"Oh Ian, I'm not paranoid about snakes but than scared the pants off me. If that had got me would I have been dead by now?"

"To tell you the truth I'm not sure. I know they are pretty deadly, so I think if he had given you a good bite, that you would certainly be unconscious and probably dead in half an hour."

Ian admired her courage as she laughed and said,

"Well my hero, I think you are entitled to a serious romp later on, if you get me out of this alive. When you said rough safari, you really meant it!" With that they continued to follow the cattle trails. They both were relieved that the bush became more open, as they left the river. They could smell the cattle now and after two hundred yards they came across an animal which could not stand and was lying in lateral recumbency. This was just what Ian needed. He unpacked his veterinary gear and while Katie held the poor animal he took blood samples and both thick and thin blood smears. He also took some smears from its lymph nodes. Katie was upset as the cow died while she was holding it still, for Ian to get the samples. He patiently explained to her that in fact the cow's death had been a mercy. Dead animals don't suffer and this poor animal had suffered enough.

He was just about to do a PM, when he thought better of it. Anyone seeing the cow as it was now would think it had just died. However if he did a PM it would be obvious that a vet had seen it and in fact some one might think he had actually killed it. He suddenly realised the danger. They were in Ethiopia. They had no business to be there. He had got the samples he required. He was pretty certain these animals were dying from Trypanosomiasis. The best thing for them to do was to get out of Ethiopia as quickly and quietly as they could and hopefully no one would know that they had been there.

Having packed up his stuff and helped Katie brush their foot prints from around the carcass they retraced their steps to the river. It took them longer, as he realised how careless he had been. They brushed their back trail as best they could. They followed the river until they came to the fresh panga cuts he had made in the trees. He was glad he knew where he was, but he was cross with himself for being such a fool to leave so much evidence. They tried to make the marks less obvious by rubbing mud on them. Then they turned for home.

They heard the soldiers some distance away. As quickly and quietly as they could, they got away from their path brushing their footprints behind them. They hid together behind a very large baobab tree. The soldiers mercifully seemed oblivious to their presence and we're talking normally. Ian did not know the language but guessed it was Aramaic.

Ian looked at Katie. She just held up her hand showing that she had got her fingers crossed.

The soldiers walked right by them. They were obviously not following Ian and Katie's tracks but just on patrol along the river.

Ian and Katie stayed in their hiding place until they could no longer hear the noise of the patrol. Then they cautiously followed their originally foot prints back the way they had come earlier in the day. They were both getting tired. They were frightened to talk in case there were more patrols. It was quite late in the day when they thought they could relax as they were back in Kenya.

They had about half an hour of light left when they reached the plane. It was just as they had left it. They made their camp again but they teased each other, as neither of them were as relaxed, as they had been on the previous night. Katie helped relieve some of the tension by stripping off and sparingly use a little water to wash herself. Then she, much to his delight insisted on washing him, as she claimed she would be much more economic with the water, and would do a much more thorough job of getting him clean.

They lit a fire and made quite a passable supper of tins of, Frankfurter sausages, whole tomatoes, bake beans, and potatoes wrapped in foil.

They discussed whether one of them should mount a guard, but decided that they wouldn't bother, as they were being ridiculous. They never did anywhere else in the NFD. They had some 'African Cream Liqueur' in their coffees and crawled into the tent. Katie laughed with Ian as she said she knew she was balmy, but she felt much safer in a tent. She said she knew he must be a little bit frightened, as he certainly was not as aroused, as normal, when he cuddled her back. Then she made him pretend that she had knickers, stockings and a suspender belt on and had asked him to take them off. Then once he had got really excited she said,

"Oh good, that little game seems to have worked, I'm going to sleep now!" Somehow Ian was not happy about that and so they had a proper cuddle and then both slept well.

Katie was delighted as they got the long flight back to Wilson Airport over in the morning and they were at Ian's home before lunch. She had a soak in the bath while Ian went to the Veterinary Laboratories.

Within ten minutes Trypanosoma vivax was confirmed, as the culprit causing the large number of acute deaths in the cattle. The DVS was pleased with the outcome and he thanked Ian. In fact he was very relieved that Ian had returned safely. When he asked Ian if he was lonely on his own in such a remote place, Ian replied,

"Not a problem, Sir. I always had the Ethiopian Army!" Ian certainly was not going to let on he took Katie.

Nelson cooked them steaks for a late lunch which they both enjoyed. Ian took Katie to Embakasi in plenty of time for her to come on duty.

Chapter 10

Ian is sent to Iran

Ian arrived at his office in good time. He had been on a successful safari. Katie was away flying and so he had been on his own. He now readily admitted to himself that he really missed her, not only on safari, but also when he was working at Kabete and she was visiting having had a few days off. He loved coming home from his office to find her at his house, particularly if she was unexpected. She often got a one night stop over. His friends, particularly his male friends adored her. It always surprised him that many of the wives of his friends enjoyed her company.

This morning he was faced with clearing the back log of files on his desk. He was not daunted. His nature was to set to and clear his desk after he had completed the report on his last safari.

He had just finished his report when he received a summons from the DVS. Normally this filled him with some trepidation, but today he did not remember anything which might earn him a bollocking. The DVS was in a relatively affable mood, but he tried to hide this, as he was always mindful that Ian was not a slave to government regulations, and wanted to keep him on his toes. He explained to Ian that he had been telephoned yesterday by the Minister of Agriculture, Bruce Mackenzie, who was his political boss. The Minister was annoyed, as he had been accosted by some horsy ladies at the Muthaiga club who had complained that the Veterinary Department were not supplying African Horse Sickness (AHS) vaccine to practicing vets, so that their horses had not been vaccinated this year. He asked Ian to explain why this was. Ian explained that in the past the Veterinary Department had always obtained a very good vaccine from South Africa, but when they came to order it this year, the Ministry of Trade and Industry had recently blocked the order, as all imports from South Africa had been banned because of apartheid. When Ian had left to go on he's recent safari, he had left Mr. Odiambo trying to find another source of vaccine. Ian said that Mr.

Odiambo had left a note on file that the only source seemed to be Iran. They appeared to have vaccine in stock, but they would not supply any trail data, nor would they supply vaccine without payment in US dollars at the time of purchase.

The DVS stroked his chin. Then he had obviously reached a decision, as he smiled,

"So Ian you had better visit Iran, check the data on the vaccine and if you think it is up to scratch, purchase some to keep the Minister happy. My PA will furnish you with the necessary documentation. Good luck."

Ian was delighted with this interview. He had always wanted to go to Central Asia. His only sadness was that he would have to go as soon as possible and therefore he would not be able to take Katie. He was not sure where she was, but recently she had been doing the long-haul direct from Heathrow to Johannesburg only stopping in Cairo. She no longer seemed to be able to get to Nairobi even for a short time. How he missed her? The longest they had ever been together was the two weeks after the hijack. That had been magic. However he had a job to do, a salary to earn and he had better get on with it or he would have the DVS after him.

East African Airways had a direct flight to Tehran and so the travel arrangements were easy. Making contact with the vaccine manufacturers who were linked to the university was not so easy, but eventually the DVS's PA managed to arrange a meeting with a Doctor Farah who said he would arrange a car to meet Ian off his flight and book him into a hotel near to the University. Finance for the trip was not a problem with the use of Government Local Purchase Orders (LPOs) signed by the DVS. However there did not seem to be a mechanism within the Kenyan Government to pay in advance. Ian imagined it would be similar to the purchase of Bull's semen for the AI Scheme. This was not the case as the AI Scheme was well known and their purchases were supplied on trust. The Iranian Authorities did not have this trust in the Kenyan Ministry of Agriculture.

The only mechanism available was for Ian to take US dollar bills. The treasury were insured for him to take up to sixty thousand pounds worth of cash. Ian knew this, as he regularly took that amount to pay for cattle in the NFD. The bank supplied an armed escort to his plane and the police in the form of the General Service Unit (GSU) would meet him at the other end.

Going to Iran, Ian would be on his own. He did not want an armed escort to his flight, as that would only draw attention to him. He therefore had to have the cash in his rucksack, as once again he did not relish having it in a briefcase chained to his arm. He definitely would rather not have his arm chopped off!

The flight was far from full and so Ian had a very pleasant seven hours reading a book. Every time an air hostess came near him, he thought of Katie, so actually he didn't read that much. Dr. Farah was good to his word and a man stood at arrivals with a sign 'Richardson' on it. The driver took him to a pleasant hotel with a nice garden. They offered him a ground floor room with a French window opening on to it. Ian declined as he was concerned about the security of the cash. He got a room on the top floor. He got room service to bring him a sandwich and some coffee to his room. He also had breakfast in his room. The reception rang him to say a car had arrived for him. Ian ascertained who had sent the car. When they mentioned a Dr. Farah, Ian was happy to go down to the lobby where his driver from the previous night was waiting for him. He was soon in Dr. Farah's office.

Dr. Farah was much younger than Ian had expected and was very excited about Ian's visit. He was very enthusiastic about his vaccine, but had the sense not to rush things and so he took Ian although the preparation and the trail work before showing Ian around the facilities. Ian was very impressed and soon realised that this Iranian vaccine was superior to the South African one.

Ian had never been a man to 'beat about the bush', so he told Dr. Farah he would buy some vaccine. The vaccine had a shelf life of five years, but as there were approximately five hundred horses in Kenya he only required two thousand and five hundred doses. Dr. Farah was very disappointed at the small number. However he was very pragmatic and thought any sale was better than no sale and so he took Ian out to lunch in a restaurant near to the airport, after Ian had paid him for the vaccine.

The vaccine was much cheaper than Ian had expected. The laboratory packed it up in a cold box all free of charge. Dr. Farah stayed with him at the airport to make sure the cold box was checked in OK. Then with a lot of handshaking he left, as Ian went through immigration.

It was in Customs where Ian's problems started. When they looked into his rucksack and found the large quantity of dollars which he had not spent, he was escorted to a small room with a table and two chairs by three officials. They laboriously counted the dollars. Ian showed them the receipt for the vaccine that he had bought and the form from the Bank of Kenya for the total amount. They agreed that the figures added up, but said that he had broken the law by not declaring the cash when he had arrived. Ian protested that he did not realise that he should have declared the cash, but this was not good enough. They said they thought he had planned to buy other DRUGs. Nothing Ian said would persuade them.

Ian knew that time was marching on. He looked at his watch and realised that his flight in theory should have left. They left him in the room having taken the cash. They gave him a signed receipt which certainly looked authentic. Ian really did think they were genuine. He never considered that they wanted a bribe. He tried to read his book but could not concentrate. He just did not know what to do.

After two hours two tough-looking men in uniform came in. They did not speak English. They indicated he should take all his clothes off and get into some rough clothing which they had brought which was obviously prison garb. All his clothes and his possessions were put in a large polythene bag. Leg chains were put around his ankles and handcuffs round his wrists in front of his body. He could now only shuffle. Ian did not try to resist, as he thought it was pointless and also would give these men some satisfaction, as they obviously wanted to give him a beating. He was pushed out the door and down a passage. As he shuffled by an open toilet he indicated he wanted to use it. He was allowed to have a wee, but the door was left open all the time.

He then had a sack type hood put over his head. Although this slightly disorientated him, he knew he had been pushed into a vehicle. It could have been a van or a small truck. He was driven for what seemed like an hour. He knew there were at least two men with him. The vehicle stopped and then backed up. The doors were opened and he was pushed out. He fell and he heard laughter. He got to his knees and then managed to stand. He was then hustled into a building. There was a lot of clanking and crashing of metal gates. He was sure he was in a prison. Eventually his hood and chains were removed. The two men left him in a cell and slammed the door as they went out. His cell was about ten foot square. It had a small bare bed and there was a bucket in a corner.

Ian sat down on the bed and took stock. He was convinced that he had only committed a minor currency crime and soon some one from the British Embassy would arrive. He knew there was no Kenyan Embassy in Tehran or the Ministry of Agriculture would have got them to purchase the vaccine. He did not feel tired. He was frustrated and annoyed. He started to pace up and down the tiny cell. He was well aware that he must not show any anger, as that would only make matters worse. He thought he should be grateful that he had not been beaten up. All he had was minor scratches on his knees, when he had fallen down.

His flight had departed. Somehow the cold box with the vaccine had gone into the hold. It was off loaded at Embakasi with the other baggage. Moses waited in the arrivals hall until there were no more passengers. He was related to one of the customs officials so he shouted to him through the arrivals door. In this way he managed to collect the cold box which was addressed to the Veterinary Laboratories. He returned to Kabete and reported to the DVS's PA. The vaccine was taken safely to the store. Neither Moses, the driver, nor the PA were really concerned that Ian was not on the flight. The DVS was in Nairobi at some important meetings and so Ian was not really missed.

It was on the following morning that the DVS sent word to Ian's office that Ian should report on his trip to Iran. Slowly his absence was realised. The DVS sent Moses to his house and Nelson confirmed that Ian had not returned. The DVS had his PA check the British High Commission; they had no news, but agreed to contact the British Embassy in Tehran. East African Airways did some checking and could find no record of Ian leaving Tehran on an East African Airways Flight.

The only other two airlines to fly into Tehran from Nairobi were BOAC and Iranian Airways. The DVS's PA checked their offices in Nairobi and they had no record of an Ian Richardson. The DVS became really concerned and put pressure on the British High Commission to make more effort to find Ian in Iran.

Eventually the Embassy in Tehran was informed that Ian had been arrested for violation of currency regulations. A junior official was despatched to the jail and was allowed to see Ian.

Having been virtually left on his own for four days, Ian had been getting more and more agitated. He was very pleased to see Timothy Taylor from the embassy. However he was not delighted when he found that Timothy did not know anything except that Ian had violated currency regulations. Ian explained exactly what had happened. Timothy looked very grave and said he would have to report back to the embassy and someone more senior would take action. Ian was far from reassured.

Meanwhile Katie arrived at his house for a forty eight hour stop over. The rest of the crew were staying at the 'Panafric'. Nelson, who looked even more worried than normal, explained to her all that he knew about Ian's disappearance. Katie had let her taxi go when she saw Ian's Landrover in the drive. However she took the Landrover up to the main office at the vet labs and went to see the DVS. Ian had introduced her to the DVS on a previous visit and so he immediately came out to his outer office, when he heard her talking to his PA. The DVS ushered her into his office and ordered a cup of tea for them both. Although Katie had come from Johannesburg she was not really tired and she looked her normal elegant self. The DVS was impressed with her appearance in her uniform. He told her all he knew which in fact was very little.

Katie could see that the DVS was, not only very concerned about Ian, but also held him in very high regard. Katie said,

"I think I had better go to Tehran. The British Government don't seem to be taking this very seriously. They certainly have dragged their feet." The DVS replied,

"That would be marvellous I will help you with any paper work which you require. However you must be careful. I don't think they treat ladies very well in Iran. If I could, I would come with you." Katie gave him a big smile saying,

"I wish you could, but I'm sure I will be OK. BOAC will help me. That is one of the perks of being an air hostess."

The DVS thought, '*Ian is a lucky man. She is so beautiful and seems so bright. I hope to goodness, neither of them gets hurt.*'

Katie broke into his thoughts,

"I wonder if your PA could get me a line to the BOAC office in Nairobi so I could sort out a flight. I think I will stay in uniform, as it will help with customs and immigration. However it would be a great help if Moses could drive Ian's Landrover and drop me at the airport and bring it home."

"Moses can take you in my staff car. He can pick you up at Ian's house when you know your flight. Then you can have time to put your feet up."

"That's really kind, but am I allowed in a government vehicle?"

"Under the circumstance that is the least I can do. I wish I had not got him into this mess. I will do anything to help you get him back to Kenya."

Soon Katie had managed to get on to a BOAC flight out of Embakasi to Tehran leaving that evening. She would be travelling in the 'jump seat'. This meant that she would be sitting on the flight deck in the seat which was no longer needed by the aircrew, as they no longer took a fourth aircrew member.

Katie managed to get through to Yvonne at the 'Panafric' and tell her what had happened. Yvonne wished her the best of luck and said she would get another air hostess to take her place. Katie really felt she was part of the team and had all of BOAC behind her.

Katie went home to Ian's house and Nelson made her lunch. She then lay out sunbathing in the garden. Normally she loved topping up her tan, but today she was so worried about Ian that she could not settle. She was even relieved to put on her uniform and be ready for Moses. He was delighted to see her, particularly as she joined him in the front of the car and inquired after his wives and children.

She had no problem with customs and immigration. She walked into the coffee shop and saw a BOAC aircrew of three guys sitting at a table reading papers. She walked boldly up to them. Her heart sank. It was Algernon's crew. However he had not forgotten the hijack. He leapt to his feet and introduced her as the bravest girl in the airline. The others all shook her hand. Katie asked if they were going to Tehran. Algernon immediately asked,

“You must be the mysterious girl who is coming with us in the jump-seat?”

So Katie told them all about Ian’s imprisonment. Algernon explained to the others that Ian had disguised himself as a Masai Moran and saved his life. Katie’s stature immediately was raised. She sat down and one of the guys quickly got her a coffee. Katie saw the cabin crew for the Tehran flight arrive. They obviously did not know who she was or why she was sitting with the flight crew. The head hostess came over. Algernon introduced Katie and said that she would be travelling in the jump-seat and to make sure she was fed with the flight-deck crew. Katie was really grateful to him and smiled to herself when she thought about his change of attitude.

The flight would have been good fun if she had not been worrying so much about Ian. However they did their best to cheer her up. In Tehran she came through immigration and customs with them without any problems. She came with them to their hotel. Algernon got her a room at BOACs expense. He laughed and said he had learnt his lesson and she had no need to sleep with the bedside lamp in her hand!

Katie was once again grateful as she was made welcome joining them all for a late supper and again at breakfast the following morning. They were then flying the Tehran to London flight. Katie left her bag at the hotel and once she had changed some money took a taxi to the British Embassy.

Things then went down hill. The receptionist was not helpful. Her problem was that although Katie had all the paperwork from Kenya, she was not Ian’s wife and she was not a Kenyan or a British civil servant. Katie thought, ‘if only I can see a man, I'm sure I will get on better.’ All she could get from the receptionist was to take a seat and when some one was free they could see if they could help her.

After about half an hour she got a break as a young man wearing a suit came hurrying out of a door marked private and went straight out of the main door. Katie was after to him in a flash. There was an embassy car waiting for him at the kerb. He was getting in the back. Katie got in the front and said to the driver, who was obviously Iranian, in her best Farsi,

“Hello. My name is Katie. What is your name?” He answered in impeccable English,

"No one at the embassy can pronounce my name so they call me Sid. You are the first person from the embassy to try to speak Farsi. I really appreciate that. Where would you like to go?"

The young man in the back was very slow off the mark, but now he lent forward and said to Katie,

"Who the devil are you?" Katie replied,

"You obviously don't understand Farsi. I have just said my name is Katie. I'm your new undercover assistant. I am disguised as a BOAC air hostess. How long have you been in Tehran?" This statement obviously totally confused the young chap. Katie gave him her most sexy smile and added,

"Don't worry I'm sure we will get along fine. I will enjoy showing you the ropes. You will love it here." He then managed,

"I've only been here a week and I have been given the task of sorting out a Kenyan who has been caught smuggling dollars out of the country."

Katie wanted to punch the air, but instead said to the driver,

"How do I say in Farsi? Please can you drive around the block and stop."Sid spoke rapidly in Farsi. Katie tried to repeat what he had said. He laughed and said it again. Katie tried again and Sid said in English,

"You have nearly got it. I will do as you ask." Katie said,

"Thank you (in Farsi)." Sid grinned and drove off. When he stopped around the corner, Katie said,

"I had better pass on my briefing to our passenger. Sorry being so rude but I ought to sit in the back. Can you carry on with the journey?"

Katie got into the back showing as much thigh as possible. She was rewarded by a distinct movement of his eyes. Undercover agent Katie then got down to work,

"So what do you like to be called?" He answered,

"Tim." Katie nearly giggled, as she thought, '*Tim nice but dim!"* However she controlled her self and replied,

"Tim it is then. Now this chap is called Ian Richardson. He is totally innocent of any charges about illegal currency. He is a very senior government vet and was sent to Iran by the Kenyan Government to buy African Horse Sickness Vaccine. So our job is to get him out of custody and send him on his way. Kenya is an ex colony and uses the British Embassy. It does not have a presence here. He has a British Passport. It should be fairly straight forward. You're the boss and should do all the negotiating. I will be in the background to support you." She crossed her legs and was glad to see he looked down. He replied,

"I'm glad he is genuine. My boss thought he was a crook and told me not to upset the Iranians as we do a lot of trade with them." Katie uncrossed her legs,

"I have had a bit of bother with your boss. I call him 'Hands', as his always seem to wander on to my thighs. What do you call him?"

"Mr. Sinclair. It would not be correct for me to call him Peregrine."

"I'll give him Peregrine, if he reaches under my skirt again!" Tim looked worried,

"That is dreadful. It must be hard being a girl." Katie moved slightly nearer to him.

"It is hard. I really need a nice kind chap like you to protect me. You are so manly." Tim went very red and did know what to say. Katie crossed her legs again.

They drew up at, what Katie thought, must be the High Security Jail. Katie thanked Sid with a beaming smile and followed Tim into the building. Things did not go well. They were not allowed to see Ian, nor were they allowed to give him any message. Katie thought Tim was a total stuffed shirt and really made no effort. She felt like kicking him, but had to keep silent. She now was really worried, as she could imagine Ian was like a caged lion and might well do something stupid. '*If only she could get a message to him, so that he would know she was in Tehran and was doing her best.*' All she could manage was to get Tim to agree to meet her at a restaurant near her hotel for dinner. She told him she would get out before they reached the embassy, as she said it was not embassy policy for her to spend anytime in the building. She thanked Sid and walked back to her hotel. The BOAC crew had checked out. She went to her room after she had done some clothes shopping. She had decided she needed to disguise herself as an Iranian.

Back in the safety of her room she stripped to her underwear and tried on her disguise. She was very pleased with it, as although she had to cover her head, her face was uncovered. It was obvious when she walked that she only had her underwear on underneath. She had seen plenty of Iranian girls in the hotel, so she thought provided she could get out of her room and get into the lift; she could then walk boldly out of the hotel. She had also bought a full burka which covered her face in case she really needed a disguise. She could in that way be totally anonymous.

As planned she was slightly late for her date with Tim, as she didn't want to be seen hanging around waiting for him. She had a real shock as he was sitting at a table with another man. She was about to leave but then she realised that he had seen her. She prayed that it was not Peregrine, as then she would be rumbled. Luckily it was a guy called John who worked for Smith Mackenzie in import/export. Katie breathed a sigh of relief.

Tim was slightly surprised that she was dressed as an Iranian, but he winked at John. Katie guessed that Tim had told him that she was his undercover assistant, so it did not really cause any problems. Katie was relieved that John seemed to know much more about Tehran. Tim had obviously told John about what he had been doing at the embassy that day. Katie could not afford to relax, but at least she could try and get some ideas as to how she could get Ian out of the country.

There was a lot of small talk. It was obvious to her that John thought she was attractive and he was much more forth coming than Tim. Katie had the impression that even if she took all her clothes off in front of Tim, he would only suggest that she might be cold!

Eventually Katie took the 'bull by the horns' and asked John if he had any ideas as to how Tim was going to get Mr. Richardson out of the country. Katie said she thought it would do Tim's career a lot of good. Tim sadly did not think it would, as Peregrine would not like it. John on the other hand wanted to impress Katie, so he was much more helpful. John said he was friendly with the Ambassador's son Richard, as they played squash together. He suggested he might help.

Katie was actually quite a good squash player so she suggested that they had a game. She did say she would be rubbish in these Iranian clothes. John laughed and said,

"No one can see into the court. We can lock the door and you can take them off."

"That sounds a brilliant idea."

So Katie agreed to meet John the following evening to play squash. She whispered to Tim that it would help with her cover and gave him the details of her hotel if he heard anything more about the Richardson case. She didn't hold out much hope, as Tim seemed so wet, but she wanted to keep as many options open as she could.

She was very depressed when she went to her room. She got room service to bring her something to eat. At least she remembered to get back into her BOAC uniform to let in the bell boy who brought the food. She did not sleep well, as she was so worried about Ian.

She woke early and had an idea. It was really only a backup plan. Her real plan was to get Richard to ask his father to pull some strings. However this other plan was to try and get Ian out of jail. She thought the authorities would have definitely kept his passport. However if she could get him a forged passport they could perhaps get out of the country. Once they were back in Kenya she was sure Ian could get a new passport.

Katie decided to see if Sid would help her. She found him outside the embassy. Sid seemed genuinely pleased to see her. She got into the front seat. She told him how Tim had been been hopeless yesterday and therefore she might have to try another approach. Had Sid any idea how she could get a forged British passport? Sid raised his eye brows,

"It would be very expensive." Katie grimaced and said,

"How much?"

"100 US."

"Oh dear that much and I think we would need two, as if we made a run for it they would have my passport details."

"The best thing for you would be to get a joint Iranian passport, as if you were husband and wife. You would not be nearly so noticeable and Iranian passports are cheaper."

Katie asked,

"Will you help me? I will make it worth your while."

"Give me 60 US and you've got a deal."

So Katie gave him her photo which had been taken when she joined BOAC. She gave him Ian's which she had always kept in her wallet. She also gave him 30 US and just hoped he wouldn't cheat her. Sid said she should come back to see him in two days.

Apparently squash was quite popular in Iran and girls did play, so Katie did not stand out in Iranian clothes. John obviously thought she was going to stand him up and so was delighted to see her. Luckily she had brought a pair of gym shoes from Kenya, as she always wore them on safari. She remembered to put on a pair of shorts and a top under her Iranian clothes. John had brought a racket for her. He was like a cat that had got the cream, as he ushered her into the court. He had a broad grin on his face when she stripped off her Iranian clothes in the safety of the court. Katie was in a dilemma, as she wanted his help to meet the ambassador's son, but she did not want him to get any other ideas.

However he seemed a gentleman. He was better than her, but not by very much and they had a good game. At the end Katie had to put her Iranian clothes back on. There was a ladies changing room so she could have a shower.

They went out of the club for something to eat. If Katie had not been so worried about Ian she would have enjoyed herself. John was good company and what was a real bonus was he said Richard the ambassador's son had said he was going to join them later, but he had to attend a function at the embassy.

Now Katie had a problem. She did not know what Tim had told John. She just hoped that her cover as an undercover assistant would stand up. It certainly wouldn't with the ambassador but it just might with his son who she gathered was only out for a visit to see his father. He was not an employee of the embassy.

Katie chatted away to John trying to get as much information about the place as she could. She felt it didn't matter that she asked a lot of questions, as she surely would be expected to do that. It sounded as if the Iranian secret police were very fierce. However they were open to bribery. If only Katie could get hold of the extra dollars which Ian had brought with him.

Richard arrived and was a little toffee nosed, but Katie thought he could be manipulated. She was at a loss as to know what he could actually do. At least he didn't blow her cover. In fact she thought he probably had never met an Iranian girl, so if he was not very bright like Tim he probably was totally confused. However Katie did her best to charm him. She was hampered because alcohol was not freely available and so the men were totally sober. Her chance came when Richard suggested they could come back to the embassy for a drink.

Katie had her heart in her mouth. She wanted to get more information, but she thought she would be in a lot of trouble if all this undercover assistant business came out. Life had been so much easier in Kenya where her good figure and short skirts seemed to have opened so many doors. She thought, '*I won't be much good to Ian if I get thrown in jail as well*'.

Katie was in a real muddle. John seemed her best ally. He certainly fancied her. So she whispered to him while Richard was organising an embassy car,

"Shall I stay dressed as an Iranian girl or shall I dress like a British girl who has just played a game of squash?" His answer did not reassure her,

"I should dress as a Brit in case we meet Richard's Father." Katie thought, '*now I'm in trouble*'. She went to the ladies in the restaurant while they were waiting for the car, and changed back into her squash gear. She would have laughed if she hadn't been so frightened. However Richard did not seem at all bothered and accepted her story that she was pretending to be an air hostess, but was really undercover.

Chapter 11

Katie meets the ambassador

They go back to the ambassador's residence. To her horror, Richard and John took her straight into the hall and there was the ambassador. John introduced her to Sir Alan Barnet. To Katie's relief he seems a genuinely caring person and shook her warmly by the hand. He asks her what she is doing in Tehran. She said she was an air hostess and worked for BOAC. He looked at her very carefully and said,

"I hope you will enjoy your time in Tehran. It is not an easy place for a young lady without a family. Please do come to me if I can be of any help to you while you are here. You must excuse me, as I have some more work to do. I'm sure Richard and John will enjoy entertaining you."

The ambassador's residence was enormous. Richard and John took Katie to the billiard room which had a full size billiard table. Once they had got drinks they tried to play snooker. It was not easy with three and Katie said,

"You two play. I saw a lovely library as we came through the residence. I will go and have a look in there."

So she left them to it. She longed to go to see Sir Alan, but her courage failed her. She sat in the library and a single tear rolled down her cheek. Then the strong Katie took over. Ian was her man. He had rescued her from the ruthless hijackers. She got up and walked boldly up to the Ambassador's study and knocked on the door. It was a solid door but she heard,

"Come in."

Sir Alan was at his desk. He had a fax in his hand and he smiled up at her as he got up.

"Let's go and sit in two comfortable chairs. I thought you might come to see me. You are a very brave and resourceful, young lady. I think you have lost something and you have come to Iran to get it back. How would you like me to help you?"

Katie's mouth dropped open and she stammered,

"How did you know?"

"It is really part of my job. When you said you worked for BOAC, I remembered the article in the Sunday Times colour supplement. I have just received this fax from the British High Commission in Kenya in reply to my inquiry, so I know rather a lot about you. Now there are some very strict rules in the diplomatic service." Sir Alan chuckled as Katie had sat down and without a thought had crossed her legs. He continued,

"I think we are just having a chat, as you are a friend of my son Richard and you have made no formal approach to the embassy." Katie blurted out,

"I'm sorry I have been really naughty."

She then told him everything she had done. He listened without interruption. When she had finished he laughed, and Katie asked why he was laughing. Sir Alan replied,

"In the nicest way I think you must be a witch. You have never met Peregrine, but I thought it was hilarious that you could invent a story about him. Shall we say I have become aware of his behaviour? However that is irrelevant. What help can I give you?" Katie replied,

"I wish I could just fly away with Ian on my broomstick. I assume normal diplomatic approaches will fail?"

"Yes, they will. He has broken Iranian law and he will be imprisoned."

Katie blinked back tears.

"I would do absolutely anything to get him out. I'm at my wits end. What should I do?"

Sir Alan got up. He walked behind his desk and must have pressed something, as a picture swung open to reveal a safe, which he opened using a combination. He took out a wad of dollar bills.

"This is my personal emergency fund. I suggest you approach Raymond Hadfield at the Sunday Times in London. He is a friend of mine. Good luck."

Katie had stood up. He handed her the money. She leant forward and kissed him on the cheek, and said,

"Thank you I won't let you down."

Katie then saw the picture which slid back over the safe. It was a picture of a BOAC air hostess very like herself. Sir Alan saw her look,

"That was my wife. She died went Richard was born. She was very similar to you."

He walked in front of her to the door and held it open, saying,

"Take care."

Katie managed once again, to travel in the jump seat on the BOAC morning flight to London. The flight deck crew were happy to have her along. Their job actually is not that glamorous and in fact, is rather boring, so a pretty girl travelling with them helps to pass the time, particularly a girl like Katie with a wealth of funny stories. Her demonstration of her finding the origin of the blood from the sick cows in Meru had them in stitches.

She was still in her uniform when she was ushered into Raymond Hadfield's office. Apparently he had played rugby with Sir Alan when they were young men. Any friend of Alan was going to be a friend of his. The fact that Katie was a very vivacious pretty girl was a bonus.

He listened to her story. Not only did he want to help her, but also he could see a great story for his paper. They hatched a plan. She was back on the evening flight to Tehran.

Sid was pleased to see her and her 30 dollars. Katie was pleased with her new passport.

Katie kept her room at the smart hotel where she was still Katie Kent, but she also took a room at a more modest hotel which was clean, but was definitely where a young wife of an Iranian business man would stay. The difficulty was the language, so she took Sid with her to book in. She wore the full hijab often called a burka, much to his amusement.

Sir Alan had briefed Peregrine and he had been instructed that the British Government were satisfied that Mr Richardson was genuine and that more vigorous efforts must be made to get him proper legal representation.

Thus Katie found herself disguised as an Iranian lawyer called Afrand Shirazi in an embassy car with Peregrine. She explained to

Peregrine that her husband Dalir Shirazi was a very jealous aggressive man. Peregrine sat as far away from her as possible!

Katie just hoped that Ian would not give her away when he recognised her.

When they reached the jail they were ushered into an interrogation room. They sat on metal chairs. Katie was appalled when Ian was brought in. He was haggard and gaunt with a rough, short, unkempt beard. He obviously had not been beaten, but had been subject to mental trauma. He was very wary. He gave no sign of recognising her, but she knew he had, as she could see that his breathing rate had risen.

Peregrine asked him if he was being fed and looked after adequately. Ian hesitated and then obviously thought there was no need to antagonise the prison staff. He just asked if he could have some reading material and be allowed to exercise in the fresh air. Peregrine was made of sterner stuff than Tim and turned to the more senior guard saying,

"Please arrange the exercise. I will bring in appropriate reading material tomorrow."

The guard just nodded, but Katie knew he had understood. Peregrine then told Ian that the British Government were acting for the Kenyan Government and both Governments were convinced of his innocence. He then introduced Katie as Afrand Shirazi who was going to be his legal representative. Katie then took over and asked that she could now be allowed to discuss the case with Mr. Richardson on her own. The senior guard said that was not allowed. Katie snapped at him,

"I'm Iranian like you. Do you want our country to be criticised by the world for inhumanity to prisoners? I must remind you that Mr. Richardson has not been tried and thus, under Iranian law, he is innocent until proved guilty."

So eventually Katie was allowed to talk to Ian alone with only one guard who sat in the corner of the room. They both were well aware that they were being monitored, but Katie could tell how just the tiniest touch, as she handed him a paper to sign, meant so much to him. It meant a lot to her as well.

When Katie left it had been agreed that she would visit on the following day.

Katie made a mental note of as much of the layout of the jail, as she could on her way out. She also walked over to the senior guard who had first been with them in the interrogation room. She wondered if he might be a candidate for a bribe. He spoke very civilly to her as she thanked him for his help. She was relieved that they spoke in English. She had bought a band of gold as a wedding ring and so she could happily say that she was recently married and did not have any children yet. It appeared he had three sons. She made a mental note of where they went to school.

Sid dropped off Peregrine at the embassy before taking her to her Iranian hotel. She slipped Sid 5 dollars and thanked him for his help. He smiled at her and said,

"You must be very careful. Trust no one. You, as a foreigner, should not have trusted me." Katie smiled at him,

"Somehow I just liked you." He laughed,

"I like you Katie or should I say Afrand. I guess Dalir is your husband who is in jail. Please be careful. May I ask how old are you?"

"I will be 19 next month." As he drew off he said,

"You are amazing. See you tomorrow."

Katie was very relieved to get to her room and relax. Her mind was in turmoil. Her main consolation was that she had at least given Ian some hope. She was amazed she was too worked up to be hungry, but she was pleased to lie on her bed. She must have gone to sleep as when she woke, it was dark. She had a bath and did her washing. She knew she would have to go out to get some food, as the hotel did not have a restaurant. She imagined Ian having dreadful food. He looked so thin. She so longed to hold him in her arms.

Her hotel was not far from a small market. Katie was enchanted by the food on display and she had no trouble buying something to keep her going that night and for breakfast the following morning. The bread was a little strange in that it was thin and came in quite large sheets. It tasted OK. She was well aware that there would be no pig products like ham for sale, but that did not worry her. She never felt threatened and she was totally left alone.

In the morning Sid came to collect her. He worried her as he said he had been told to bring her to the embassy before he took her to the jail, as there had been some new developments. He did not know what they were. Katie just prayed that Ian had been released. Her hopes were dashed when she was ushered into Peregrine's office. He said that the Iranian customs had arrived as soon as the embassy opened. They presented him with all the dollars which they had taken off Ian at the airport. They gave him photocopies of the various bills that Ian had shown to the authorities. Peregrine said they all seemed to be correct. He asked Katie what he should do now. Katie asked if Sir Alan had been informed. Peregrine said he did not want to bother Sir Alan. Katie said she totally understood, but she thought Sir Alan would like to be kept up to date with developments. Katie suggested that with Sir Alan's permission she thought the currency should be returned to Kenya in the diplomatic bag, as it was Kenyan and not British money. She told Peregrine that she was not sure whether this gesture was good or bad news. On the one hand she thought it was good news as the authorities here in Iran were sticking to international law. On the other had she thought it was bad news, as she thought, as they had not released Ian that they were still going to charge him with currency regulations violations?

Of course Peregrine thought Katie was Afrand. He was reluctant to go to the Ambassador on the request of an Iranian lawyer. However Peregrine thought she was very pretty and therefore wanted to be in her good books. Therefore he approached the ambassador at the embassy. He was surprised that Sir Alan was not upset by having to deal with such a relatively minor problem. Sir Alan said,

"What do you think Peregrine?"

"I think it shows sound judgement."

"Good, therefore we will run with it. Keep me up dated."

Katie was pleased when Peregrine informed her. She asked that an official receipt was obtained from the Kenyan Government as that would strengthen her client's case.

Sid took her to the jail. Katie was pleased that the senior prison officer who she had spoken to on the previous day greeted her affably and took the trouble to accompany her to the interrogation room.

Ian was brought in. Katie was still terribly worried about him. Obviously he could not show how pleased he was to see her, but it was his hollow cheeks and sunken eyes which disturbed her. The only thing which cheered her was that he was certainly not giving his guards any concerns that he had any ideas of trying to escape. She just hoped he was a better actor than she imagined he was. She asked him if he had been allowed to exercise outside. He said they had allowed him out of his cell for an hour, but only in a courtyard with very high wall. He had not been allowed to meet any other in mates. The senior prison officer butted in saying,

"It is only for his safety. I'm concerned that other Iranian inmates might attack him." Katie wanted to try and get a dialogue with this man, so she said,

"That's kind of you and I'm sure my client is grateful for your help. However I see no reason from a legal standpoint, why he should be in solitary confinement. Are there not some less aggressive prisoners that he could mix with, when he is out on exercise?"

The senior prison office scratched his head and said,

"If you make a specific request, I suppose he could be allowed to mix with some Kurdish prisoners who are being held on treason charges." Katie answered,

"That is most helpful. After I have had a one to one with my client, may I come to your office and draft the formal request?" She turned to Ian and said,

"Now Mr Richardson I have brought you some books which I hope you will find interesting. We will sit together in this corner and start to prepare your defence. Your jailers have been most helpful. We need to prepare an argument. We need to convince a judge of your innocence."

So Katie and Ian sat close together in a corner with a guard looking on. It was agonising for both of them. However Katie used the time wisely. She very carefully used various bits of sign language to get Ian to understand how she was going to use the books as a method to communicate with him in a simple book-code. Obviously nothing could be written. However she could use a pin so he could follow the code. She left two copies of one book, so he knew which one to use. She would take one copy away the next day so that the guards would not guess. She had great difficulty not to weep when she left him. However she steeled herself and made her way to the senior prisoner's office.

He obviously fancied her and offered her some tea which she accepted. She asked him about his family. She got him to help her to draft the official request, for Ian to be allowed to mix with other prisoners. Katie was suddenly at a loss as to how to behave in her new persona. Life was so much easier in a short skirt and a low top. She sensed that this might be her only chance. She crossed her legs which generated a rustle of silk. She fluttered her eyelashes and their hands touched as he held the paper for her. Katie realises it is now or never. Her hand slipped on to his knee. He did not remove it, so she said,

"I will look forward to seeing you tomorrow."

"I will look forward to seeing you Afrand."

"What is your name?"

"It is Aga."

"Goodbye until tomorrow Aga."

She got up and he escorted her from the jail.

She got Sid to drop her off on the way back so she could do some shopping. She said she would walk back to the hotel. One of her purchases was going to be a good map of Tehran and also a map of the west of Iran.

When she got back to her hotel she drew a map of all she could remember about the layout of the jail.

She also made a list of things she would require. The plan she had concocted with Raymond Hadfield was simple enough. However Katie knew that detailed planning was vital.

In the morning Sid took her to the jail as normal. Aga had sent word to the guards that she was to be escorted to his office first before she saw the prisoner. Katie was a bag of nerves. However she walked boldly into his office. He immediately got up from behind his desk and greeted her formally before dismissing the guard. She knew what was going to happen when he walked to the door and locked it, saying,

"Now we can be more private."

Katie had read somewhere that if you smiled your voice on the telephone became friendlier. Was it the same if you were wearing a burka? She willed a smile, and asked,

"You have something private to tell me?" She crossed her legs. They both were well aware of the sound of the silk. She was expecting a sexual advance but was surprised when he said,

"I gather the dollars which were found on the prisoner have been sent by the customs office to the British Embassy." Katie had to make massive effort not to let her breath out in a rush. '*Thank goodness he was after a bribe.*' She replied,

"So I understand. I was wondering if some of the money could be given to you so that you could make my client's life a bit better. He does not look very well."

"That sounds an excellent plan. I am in a position to do just that." Katie replied,

"You are so helpful I'm glad we understand each other." She looked him in the eye and added,

"I haven't got any of that money, as it is at the embassy." A slight frown crossed his face. She continued,

"I have a little of my own money which I can give you and then indent to the Embassy." He smiled. He smiled even wider when Katie, very discretely reached under her long covering and withdrew some notes which had been in her stocking tops. She thought, '*Thank goodness for a suspender belt.*'

She was soon in the interrogation room with a bored guard and Ian who thanked her for the books. He said he was returning one as he had been reading avidly. Katie said she was pleased as she had brought two more. They chatted some more with Ian managing to give her more information, like the time of the meals, the time of his exercise etc.

They were both sad when she had to go, but Katie could tell how much happier Ian had become. She just prayed that the guard would not notice.

When she got back to the hotel and deciphered his coded message, she was secretly pleased as he had said such lovely things about her. However the practical Katie thought, '*He is such a Wally. Thank goodness I grilled him. Fond endearments are not going to get him out of jail.*'

She relented when she wrote back, as she knew she must keep his spirits up. She also realised how foolish she had been writing things down. Luckily she had a good memory, so she used it and flushed all the notes, after she had put a match to them, down the toilet.

Over the next few days Ian managed to give her quite a large amount of information about the Kurdish prisoners. Katie for her part gave some more dollars to Aga. She was honest with herself. She knew that Ian meant so much to her that she would have granted the man sexual favours, but she was very relieved that it did not seem to be necessary.

Every day in the car she chatted to Sid. She did not say anything to him, but she was delighted when he told her that he was a Kurd and that his family lived in Eastern Turkey.

She divided her time between the two hotels. She told the posh European Hotel that she had been flying. She told the Iranian Hotel that she spent some time with her family.

One morning she received a friendly note via Sid from the Ambassador saying he was wondering how she was getting on and asking her for supper at the Residence.

She arrived in smart European clothes and was shown into his study. When they were alone she told him exactly what had been happening. She did not spare him any details and told him how nervous she was about whether the bribe was going to be her body or money. When he looked aghast, she said,

"I'm sure your wife would have done it for you. In fact you are such a lovely man I would do it for you."

He had a tear in his eye as he got up and stroked her neck saying,

"I'm sure she would have. I would be very proud if you were my daughter. However now we must get down to business. I gather that Raymond is now in Tehran. I think it would be better if he contacted you at the airline hotel. I hope you both won't need it, but you know you always can come here if things are really desperate." Katie answered,

"I would hate to compromise you."

"Rubbish, you are the daughter that I never had. Now we must have something to eat. Let me lead you through to the dining room." It seemed natural for her to take is arm. They talked enjoyably throughout the meal. Katie had him in stitches telling him about her adventures. He kept her enthralled about the country of Iran and the

Iranian people. They finished in his study with a cup of coffee before he said,

"Katie, look how late it is. Now you must go." He went with her to the door. As she kissed him on the cheek he said,

"Good luck Katie. Remember you are the best."

Chapter 12

The plan comes to fruition

In the morning she went to the airline hotel and changed into Katie the air hostess. She went to the BOAC office to leave a note for Raymond Hadfield. She was in luck as he was in the office asking for her. Over coffee he brought her up to date with everything from his end. He was pleased that she had got a direct lead into Ian and had bribed the senior prison officer. They worked out some more exact plans. They had a deadline, as the Kurdish prisoners in the jail were due to be tried for treason which carried the death penalty, on the 3rd June. A demonstration was planned for the 1st June. The break out was planned to take place on that morning. Raymond had been organising bus loads of Kurds to come into Tehran. They would be camping outside the jail on 31st May and would act as a diversion. Katie had a lot to accomplish.

Her regular meetings with not only Ian, but also Aga continued. Katie could see that the man found her attractive, but she needed to get on another level of friendship. She decided to up the bribe so she casually said,

"I will be guided by you, as you have been so kind. You suggested that other prisoners might harm my client. I am concerned that, as you are getting him better food, they might find out and there might be some jealousy. You said he exercises with Kurdish prisoners. Would it help if I gave you a little more money to help with their food?" He replied,

"That would be difficult for me as it would show favouritism."

"Surely you are very senior and you could treat them as one group?"

"You are a very kind young lady but it is not simple as I am a Kurd, but of course loyal to the government." Katie thought,

'That is marvellous news.' She said,

"I entirely understand. Perhaps it would be possible for me to distribute the food if I was monitored by one of your more junior colleagues in the same way that I can bring books to my client. The British Embassy is concerned for his safety, so I'm sure they would be happy for your remuneration to be increased."

"I would be worried for your safety."

"You are a kind thoughtful man, but you must not let my sex be a consideration. The British Government hold your countrymen in very high regard. So do I. They have never been found guilty in a court of law and therefore I am happy to trust them." He replied,

"You have my admiration."

So the following day Katie arrived at the jail with more dollars in her stocking tops and a large food parcel of food which Aga had suggested. The fifteen Kurdish prisoners as well as Ian were surprised to see her in the exercise yard. Katie however explained the position. It seemed to be acceptable to them. She also had requested in code from Ian that he gave her a list of small items which she could hide either in the food or on her person which would aid their breakout.

From then on her visit became routine. Neither the food nor her person was searched. She had a meeting with Raymond and he said he would try and get her two small revolvers. He teased her saying he wondered if she needed any help taping them to her inner thighs. Katie laughed saying,

"Dream on Raymond." Then she made him laugh telling him about where Ian's face had ended up on the first time she drove him on safari. She made Raymond promise to reimburse Sir Alan's emergency fund. He teased her again and said he would take it out of the royalties she had accrued from her full frontal in his paper. They agreed to meet one more time before the 1st June. Raymond handed over the two pistols and an envelope from Sir Alan.

Katie opened it when she was in the safety of her modest hotel room. There was no note but it contained two new passports. One was a replacement for Ian's which was being held by the Iranian authorities. The other was in the name of Mrs Katie Julie Richardson. There was also a marriage certificate dated in the week following the hijack attempt. Katie could not stop crying because of

Sir Alan's kindness. It made her even more determined to get Ian out of Iran and back to safety.

She had checked out of the airline hotel the previous day without any problems. On that day she also smuggled the pistols into the jail. On the morning of the 1st June, she stopped into the office of the other hotel. She did not check out but settled her account up to date. She just hoped that she would not be coming back.

Sid took her to the jail as normal. The area was full of Kurdish protesters. She told Sid to return to the embassy, as she said it might be dangerous for him to wait. She said she would get the jail to ring the embassy when it was safe for him to come and pick her up. She called into Aga's office with the normal money and with food parcel. To her relief he did not accompany her to the exercise area, as he said he needed to be beside a telephone in case the situation outside of the jail got out of hand.

When she was being shown into the exercise yard pandemonium erupted. She was not quite sure what happened. The two guards were over powered. She was thrown to the floor and her arms were taped actually very loosely behind her back. She saw that they had also done the same to Ian. There was a lot of shouting in a language which she guessed was Farsi. She was hauled to her feet and frog marched by two prisoners into a passage. One had a pistol at her head. At the end of the passage she could see other guards backing away from them.

Then there was a terrific explosion behind her. Her and her capturers were thrown forward on to their knees. A voice shouted in her ear,

"Turn around we must move quickly, our friends have blown the wall." Katie was slightly dazed, but did as she was told. She thought she recognized Ian ahead of her. Then there were gun shots. Katie knew they were too loud to be from the pistols so they must be from the guards. As she was dragged out into what was left of the exercise yard there was more shouting and the pistol was held again held at her head.

Katie was relieved that she could now see Ian also with a pistol at his head, being dragged up a heap of rubble which had been a wall.

The other Kurds were climbing as quickly as they as they were able. Her captor said quietly as he cut her bond,

"Pretend to limp. Put your arm around my neck and act dazed." He then screamed something in Farsi when one of the guards fired a shot.

Slowly he dragged her up the rubble using her as a shield and keeping the pistol on her head. At the top he just dived backwards still holding her but with the pistol held away. They both fell on to several mattresses on a small lorry which accelerated away. The back of Katie's head had hit his chin. She really was dazed, but as she rallied she realised that she had actually knocked out her captor who was considerably more dazed than her. They were alone in the back of the lorry. She knew they were very exposed so she started to haul him under one of the mattresses. It was very difficult as the lorry was bouncing around and he seemed a dead weight.

Eventually she managed it and just lay beside him gasping for breath. At least she thought they were now hidden from view from the windows. When she felt stronger she shook him shouting,

"Wake up. I'm sure we will have to change vehicles soon?" He said something in Farsi. Katie thought, '*I know I shouldn't shake him but I don't think he is concussed, as I think it was the back of my head which caught him under his jaw.'*

She shook him again. She remembered her brothers being knocked out playing rugby. She shouted,

"What day of the week is it?" He replied in Farsi. Katie shouted,

"What's your name?"

"Ajar."

"Speak English Ajar. What's the plan? I knocked you out by mistake, when we fell into the lorry." He shook his head,

"I thought I was in paradise." Katie laughed,

"I'm certainly not one of your virgins. Anyway I suspect shagging virgins is an overrated pastime. I'm Afrand but my really name is Katie. We must get out of this lorry. The police will have its number by now."

Ajar shook his head. Katie was not sure whether it was because he was still dazed or whether Kurdish girls did not treat their men quite like she was treating him. She was lying on top of him clinging on to the side of a mattress under another mattress. They were bouncing about violently. He managed,

"Apo, the driver knows where he is going." Katie did not let up,

"What's the plan?" Ajar smiled,

"Where is that pistol?"

With one hand, Katie retrieved it from between the mattresses and held it to him with an enquiring look." He gave another smile.

"I was going to hold it to your head to shut you up! You were a marvellous submissive girl in the prison."

"I'll give you submissive girl! That was just an act. You great Wally."

"What's a Wally?"

"A bloody fool." Ajar laughed and then regretted it, as obviously his head hurt.

"I'm the leader. You, as a woman, just do as you are told." It was Katie's time to laugh,

"I've got news for you chum. All the important men in my life treat me as an equal." She held out her hand and losing balance as the lorry bounced, fell on top of him. His arm went around her,

"I have never met anyone like you Katie. All I can say is Ian is a lucky guy but I can see that you are not going to be as the Americans say, 'a push-over'!' Now we must be quick."

The lorry was slowing. He did not hear her reply of,

"I'll give you a bloody push-over!"

She was over the side before him, ripping her covering. She followed Apo who was getting into a Landrover. She got into the middle seat. She was not sure whether Apo was impressed with her legs or the wad of dollars taped to her thigh. However Katie thought, '*Now I'm really on home ground.*'

Apo let in the clutch, as Ajar got in beside her. Katie asked,

"How far are we behind the others?" He replied,

"Not many minutes but we are split into two groups. We will join the back group. Ian is more important and he is in the front group. Katie chucked her head. The effect was rather lessened as her head was still covered. She took off the covering and shook out her hair. She saw his eyes go down to her legs and the money. She said,

"Both are off limits." Ajar nodded his head and then could not stop himself shaking his head as she made no effort to cover her stocking tops.

No more was said. Apo drove fast but sensibly. Katie was aware that before they had been travelling north, but now they were on a more westerly direction. It was not a major road but the surface was good. They went steadily for over an hour and Katie was getting sleepy when they saw a man running towards them. Apo did a quick three point turn and the man clambered in the back. There was a lot of Farsi. Eventually, Ajar said,

"There is a road block. We will go another way." Katie asked,

"Did the others get through?"

"Yes. Sadly we will have a much harder climb. Will you be up to it?" He put his hand on her thigh. He expected her to slap his hand. Instead she eye-balled him and said,

"I know we have agreed that my thighs are off limits, so as I know you are a man of your word, I took that as a kind encouragement. He removed his hand with a tiny stroke,

"You are a very remarkable young lady. Of course I will give you all the encouragement that I can."

Soon they turned left on to a more northern heading. The road became rougher and they were obviously climbing. Then the road ended in a small glade. Ajar turned to Katie,

"Now you have a choice. Apo and this other man are not known to the authorities. They will ditch the vehicle and get back to their homes. I'm a marked man and will go on from here on foot. You can go with them and hope that the authorities will accept your story that you are an innocent lawyer, when you give yourself up, or you can come on with me." Katie did not hesitate,

"I will come on with you."

However she thought, '*that is not the only option. I could go on alone. I'm going to hold this guy up. He has a better chance on his own. Why am I so stubborn? The authorities are definitely going to put me in jail. My sensible option is to get to the Embassy and get Sir Alan to get me out. However I feel I am betraying him, as the whole business is going to look very bad and it will ruin his career.*'

Ajar replied,

"I am the leader. You will have to do what I tell you."

"Fine but my thighs are still off limits but the money will be communal."

Apo found her a small rucksack with water, some biscuits, a compass and a light blanket. Already Ajar had started up the path. Katie thanked Apo and set off after Ajar. She took off all her Iranian clothes and stuffed them in the rucksack as she climbed up after him. She thought she looked a real trollop so she stopped and took off her stockings and suspender belt and stuffed them together with the money into the rucksack. Mercifully it still was not heavy. Katie did not try to catch up Ajar but paced herself. She did manage not to let him get any further ahead.

He did not stop. Eventually as dusk was falling she was having difficulty following him. She did not notice when he stopped and she walked straight into him. He held her and said,

"We will have a break now and then continue when the moon comes up."

He sat down and ate some biscuits and drank some water. Katie said,

"I'm well aware that I am going to hold you up, but if I can stay with you until the morning, that would be really kind. Then you must go on alone and I will do the best that I can on my own." She felt his hand on her thigh as he said,

"I have not forgotten that it was you that engineered our breakout. I know it was for Ian but you have helped me and my men. We will go on together. I know most girls would be terrified to be out on these mountains alone with a man, but somehow I don't think you are. You fascinate me. Ian is a lucky man. I will do my best to return you to him."

His hand was still on her thigh. She squeezed it, but made no effort to remove it. She asked,

"In the UK or in Kenya when a girl gets married, she often has another girl called a bridesmaid to support her. Do Kurdish girls do the same?" He replied,

"Yes they do. Why do you ask?"

"I'm going to be on the lookout for a wife for you. It would be good if we could be friends."

"You are a strange girl Katie. How do you know that I haven't got a girl already?"

"I don't think you have thought about a wife in your life up to now, but my thighs have made you consider having one." Ajar laughed,

"Any man would want to put his hand on your thigh." It was Katie's turn to laugh.

"I might agree with that, but you don't just want to touch my thighs, you want to possess them. It is a different thing altogether."

They said no more until the moon just rose and he got up. He put everything in his rucksack. Katie was grateful and did not try to stop him. Then they set off.

Katie thought she was fit but this was something else. She just would not give in and kept doggedly following him. It was getting colder so at least she was keeping warm. Just when she thought she was totally finished and would have to ask him to stop they came to a shepherds hut. It was just a stone hovel but at least in was dry and she thought it was much better than sleeping outside. They had good night vision. He gave her all her clothes from the pack. Katie said,

"I know I should not ask, but can we sleep together to try and keep warm?"

"Of course that would be sensible."

They both had a wee outside the hut. Katie pulled up her short skirt and but on her suspender belt and stockings and then pulled her skirt down. She wrapped her Iranian cloak around her. She said,

"Let's sleep on one of the blankets. You lie on you back and I will lie on top of you. Then you bring the other blanket over top of us both." He asked,

"Where do I put my hands?"

"On my bottom."

"Doesn't that mean I want to, in your words, possess it."

"Yes it does, but I think you value my friendship higher than my body."

"Yes I think I do, but it is going to be hard."

"It's going to be hard for me. You are a very attractive man."

Because they were so tired, sleep came quickly.

Katie was aware that he was awake, so she rolled off him. He said,

"It is just dawn. I will check carefully outside to see we are alone. Then we will leave. We will break to eat later."

He came back in when Katie was just in her knickers as she had taken off her stockings.

"Is it OK if I go outside to have wee?"

"Yes. We appear to be alone."

Katie was quick. She came back into the hut and pulled on her skirt and shoes, while he was filling his rucksack. Then they were off. He set a brisk pace to try and warm them up. They both kept a constant lookout, but they saw no one. The valley that they were climbing in seemed to be totally empty. Katie was relieved when they reached the head of the valley where there was a small group of stunted trees. They were fortuitous as that meant that they were not on the sky line as they crossed into the next valley. They stopped for some food. Katie did not go far and went to the loo. She was grateful for her Kenyan training. She was crying when she came back to him. He mistook the cause and said,

"I am sorry it is so humiliating for you." Katie smiled,

"It is not that. I was just remembering when I first went on safari with Ian. I hope he and the rest of your men have got away OK."

Ajar put his arm round her.

"I pray for that as well."

"Have you ever slept with a girl before?"

"No it would not be allowed." She teased him, saying,

"You will be able to say to your men, that I was a good lay."

"I will never say anything like that. I would only say how marvellous you were when I held a loaded pistol to your head."

"Thank you. A kind statement like that was like a stroke on the thigh."

"Come we must keep going or you will say I want to possess your shoulder!" He took his arm from around her with a lot of reluctance.

Losing some height made the going a little easier but it was harder on Katie's knees. She was so grateful to her Kenyan 'tackies' as she did not have any blisters.

They came to a small stream which they crossed. Ajar made her take off her shoes and walk up the stream for over a hundred yards, following him, as he said it would confuse tracker dogs if the authorities were after them. They kept going all day. Once again Katie was getting very weary as they climbed out of yet another valley.

Suddenly Ajar stopped and ordered her to stand still. He slowly put his hands into his pockets. Katie remembered 'Boy' so she slowly crossed her arms over her chest. Two of the most enormous dogs bounded up to them. They wore thick leather collars with large metal studs. They snarled and slowly came towards them crouching. Katie did not move a muscle. She watched as one came up close to Ajar and snapped threateningly in his groin. The second came up to her and slowly moved its wet nose up under her skirt. It just licked her knickers and she just stood there crying. Then there was shouting and the dogs turned and ran to the voice. Ajar went to comfort Katie, only to find her smiling. He was perplexed,

"Why did you cry?"

"Happy memories, I will explain to you sometime."

He shook his head, turned and carried on walking. They met an old man with the dogs walking beside him to heel. Ajar knew the man and they embraced. He introduced Katie and the man said something which Katie did not understand. Ajar translated.

"He said this woman is lucky that his dogs did not rip her apart." Katie slowly knelt on to her knees and reached a hand slowly up to each dog. They gently licked her hands. Katie said,

"Can you tell him that I like dogs and usually they like me." The dogs continued to lick her hands as the two men conversed. Katie slowly came off her knees and started walking down the track. She could see the man's hut in the distance. Every so often she felt a wet nose on her thigh under her skirt. The men stayed talking for a few minutes and then followed her.

At the hut Ajar said, "Armanc says I can stay in his hut tonight, but that it is not Godly for you, as a woman, to share a hut with two men." Katie replied,

"Please tell him I totally understand and that I am very grateful for any help he can give us. I can see the two dogs sleep in that kennel over there. Could I sleep with them, as I will be very cold otherwise?"

Obviously Armanc was very worried and said something which Katie was sure meant, 'What is the world coming to. I meet an almost naked girl and she wants to sleep with my dogs!'

The two men continued to talk so Katie walked about fifty yards away to a small stream. The dogs followed her. She found a big rock so that she was out of sight. She took off her clothes and sat in the freezing cold water. It made her catch her breath but it was very refreshing. Having washed she got out and sat on a warm rock with her back to the big rock. There was some warmth in the sun. She dozed off to sleep.

She woke, as Ajar cleared his throat. He had great difficulty dragging his eyes away from her. She talked as she dressed,

"Don't worry Ajar. I don't mind that you have seen me naked. The swim was lovely and refreshing. If I did not think it would have worried Armanc, I would have asked you to join me."

"Oh Katie, how do you expect me, not to want to possess you? I don't expect you to wear the full hijab in the hills, but ...." His voice tailed off. He did not know what to say.

Supper was very nourishing. It was mutton stew followed by yoghurt and honey. Katie took the dogs for a short walk and then happily went to bed with them in their kennel after Ajar had given her a blanket. The dogs were lovely and warm. They kept licking her face but actually she had a good nights sleep.

They left in the morning after a big mug of tea, with lots more yoghurt and honey. It was obvious that Ajar had things on his mind, so Katie just followed steadily behind him. He turned to her after an hour or so and said,

"Can we talk?" Katie came up beside him saying,

"How can I help?"

"I feel so embarrassed about you having to sleep with those dogs."

"Don't worry about it. I had a good night's sleep."

"I have been worried about, seeing you naked."

"Oh dear, am I that ugly?"

"Oh Katie please be serious. You are too beautiful, but it was wrong of me. I somehow knew you would be swimming. I felt like a voyeur but I just could not stop myself."

"Look Ajar. You must not worry. If it is cold tonight, I will still want to cuddle up to you to keep warm. You know Ian is my man. You have accepted that, so you have no need to worry."

"Were you really so terrified of those dogs that you burst into tears and yet you were happy to share a kennel with them?"

Katie really laughed then, as she told him about all the happy times she had in Meru Game Park. He looked appalled when she told him about a fully grown lion licking her. He looked even more appalled when she said that if she hadn't been so terrified she would have enjoyed it. He said,

"Katie that is so bad and wrong."

"We will have to agree to disagree. I don't think it is wrong to be honest about what you feel and what you like. I would not let an animal lick me on purpose as that would be debasing the animal but when Ian licks me that's wonderful." Ajar stopped walking and said,

"Can we never mention it again?"

"Of course, I won't."

They walked on in silence for the rest of the morning. It was only when they stopped for lunch that Ajar opened up and answered Katie's questions on what their plans were.

All that afternoon they continued to climb to the head of the pass. Katie was worried as it was definitely getting colder.

They got to the top and there was a spectacular view of crop growing countryside. She could make out what looked like dwellings. They started to descend and it rapidly became warmer although evening was upon them. Katie could see a wide river. It separated them from this flatter land which was obviously very fertile. She asked Ajar,

"Is that the Ghezel Ozan River?"

"Yes, we must cross it this evening. We will be much safer on the other side as all the populous are Kurds."

"Is there a bridge?"

"No, but hopefully we can get a boat."

Somehow they were both worried that pursuit was catching up with them. They wanted to cross the river that night. It was dusk when they reached a small village with a landing stage. On the outskirts of the village, Ajar made he put on her burka, but not a full hijab. There were no boats. Apparently all the boats stayed on the other side at night. There was an old man who had a canoe, but he did not want to go over that night. Katie whispered to Ajar,

"Why don't we buy it off him? We can sell it on the other side."

So a deal was struck. There were two paddles. Katie was used to water and was a good swimmer. She had never really been able to master canoeing really well, but she had hired them with her brothers when they were children. She immediate flagged up Ajar's unease. Her bossy BOAC training came to the fore and she hustled him along. They soon had the canoe in the water. They got on fairly well in the still water near the bank and as they relaxed they picked up the rhythm. Then Katie had a thought about what would happen if they got all their things wet. She made Ajar return to the bank and she put the vital things into a polythene bag and then put this small bundle in a second bag. They she put the whole thing in her small rucksack on her back.

They set off again. Only when they were a considerable distance from the bank did Katie ask him if he could swim. His reply was ,

"Not very well." This did not encourage her, she said,

"If we capsize you just hold on to the boat. I will swim around and sort everything out. At least I am happy as we have the vital things in my rucksack on my back."

They paddled on. It was really getting dark, but they could see the lights on the opposite bank. Sadly they did not seem to be getting any nearer. Katie remembered from the map that she had bought in Tehran that it was a wide river. She just hoped that like many wide rivers there was no strong current. She thought of Africa. She did not think there were any hippos or crocs here.

They kept paddling on. Katie then realised that the current was becoming stronger. She knew that they must not try to fight it, but just to go at angle across it. Then suddenly they hit the main current. Ajar said,

"I don't like this. We ought to turn back." Katie tried to reassure him,

"I think that would be more dangerous. We will keep paddling and go with the flow and slowly edge our way across."

Because he was nervous, Ajar kept missing his strokes. Katie kept trying to encourage him. She genuinely was not scared. She knew when she first saw the river that she could actually swim across.

Then disaster happened. Ajar missed his stroke, tried to compensate and over they went.

He let go of the canoe and his paddle and grabbed Katie. He was maniacal. He clutched at her clothing which ripped. Katie's first thought was, '*good riddance, it will make swimming easier.*

Mercifully her rucksack was firmly on her back, both over her shoulders, round her waist and there was even a small strap high up across her chest. He got a grip on her bra and Katie realised that radical action was required. She managed to kick out with her legs to separate him from her and then she hit him hard with the paddle. That had the desired effect. He was knocked out. She rolled him on his back and started life saving him, as she had been taught at school.

All the time they were being swept along by the current. They were lucky as, when they had capsized they were over the main stream and so the current now helped her to get him to the shore. He kept coughing so she knew he was still alive. It was a hard swim for her, but she had strong legs and each kick in her mind brought her nearer to the bank. It never occurred to her to leave him and save herself. At last she felt sand below her. She kept swimming and then, not only did she feel sand with her feet, but also on her bottom.

She managed to stand and pull him on his back through the shallow water.

She could smell sheep and goats. She had obviously come to a watering place. She dragged him up on to the grass bank and rolled him on to his front. When she hit him on his back, he coughed violently. Then he vomited up some river water. He started breathing normally. She felt his head. There was an egg-sized lump on the side of his head just in front of his ear. She thought, '*I hope I didn't hit him too hard and that I have given him brain damage.*'

As they were much lower down the temperature was not cold. She was not even shivering. The ebullient Katie showed it's self. She thought, '*Ian would be proud of me. I'm dressed in some skimpy knickers and some tackies in a country where every other girl is clothed from head to toe and I don't give a damn.*'

Then she heard the tinkle of bells. The sheep and goats were coming down for their evening drink. Then the dog smelt her. He barked and she saw his teeth in the gloom. She stood totally still with her hands by her side. There was someone with a light behind him. It reflected on the studs of his collar. He came boldly towards her. His head was held high and was at the level of her breasts. He stopped and sniffed her. Katie thought, '*I think he would attack if he smelt perfume or make up, but all he can smell is river water.*'

It was a standoff. They both stood still. The lights were being carried by two lads in their early teens. Katie thought, '*They probably think I'm a ghost or a river nymph.'*

They just stood and stared. Katie was reluctant to speak as she thought speech might provoke an attack by the dog, so she took George Adamson's lead and slowly reached down and fondled the dog's ears. It slowly became submissive. She slowly sank onto her hunches and it layed its massive head on her lap. She gently held its collar.

Suddenly it was all too much for the boys. They turned and fled. The dog stayed with her so she reached down for Ajar's belt and used it as a lead. Ajar was still unconscious but breathing normally with his head in the proper recovery position. With the dog trotting beside her, she started walking along the bank in the same direction that the boys had taken.

She smiled when she thought what a strange sight she must make. She was sure Raymond would have liked a picture for his paper. Perhaps Algernon had been right. Maybe she would have been better as a model.

She could hear voices coming towards her. The dog growled and gave a single bark. The chattering continued. There were several strong torches. Soon the beams found her and there was silence. Katie then had a horrendous vision of being stoned to death. She stood her ground. This was the Katie who had defied a hijacker who had just shot two of the crew. She took strength from her inner self and from the dog pressed against her. A male voice shouted something in Farsi. The dog growled. Katie gentled it and called back in Farsi,

"Hello, can you help?" There was silence. Then she tried English,

"Can you help?" They a voice said,

"Are you a fairy?" Somehow this amused Katie and she smiled,

"Do I am just an English girl who fell in the river. My friend needs help, as he nearly drowned. I will show you."

She turned and walked with the dog back to Ajar. She sensed that they were following. Ajar had recovered consciousness and was sitting with his head in his hands moaning. He looked up in horror. Katie was not sure whether it was because she was virtually naked of because of the men following her.

She said,

"How do you feel? You nearly drowned. Do you remember anything?"

"I am so sorry. I remember fighting with you trying to keep afloat and ripping your clothes." Katie laughed,

"You did a good job of that."

"Then everything is blank until I woke up here."

"I had to control you, so I hit you on the head with the paddle and then swum with you to the bank. Are you strong enough to talk to these people and see if they will help us?

Ajar got groggily to his feet and started talking to the men behind her.

The dog obviously liked her and just stood beside her pressed up against her. The dog was a great comfort to her, as she found it very harrowing, just standing being stared at. Then a smile came on her face, as she thought it was much easier for strippers as they could do sexy dances. Then she remembered her mother saying that she and her father had gone with a group of friends to the 'Windmill Theatre' in London before the war. Her mother had said it was hilarious that the stripper, 'Peaches Western' had to stand still when she was naked, then the lights would go out. She then had to do another pose and then the lights came back on! Girls with no clothes on were not allowed to be seen to move.

Katie must have communicated her thoughts, as very slowly a teenager had come forward with his shirt. She thanked him in Farsi. She took off the rucksack and put on the shirt.

Ajar came to her then, saying that they were being welcomed into the village. As he walked beside her he said,

"Thank you for saving my life. The villagers say that no man has ever swum across the river since the days of 'Alexander the Great'. They are in high approbation of you." She answered laughing,

"Have you ever torn a girl's clothes off before?"

"Of course I haven't."

"Well you did a good job."

"Oh Katie you must not tease me."

That night they were found separate accommodation. Katie gave Ajar most of the stuff out of the rucksack, just keeping some money and the passports which she had acquired. She was glad to give him the pistol. She lodged with a young widow who had three daughters who were in their early teens. Katie was delighted as the girls could speak English. Their mother was a kind woman and in fact was hardily older than Ian. It appeared that her father was the most senior man in the village and so she was not bowed down by the cares of the world. Once the girls had got over their initial shyness they were very forth coming. A copper bath was prepared so Katie could have a really good soak. There was no shyness and they all watched her. Their mother explained that her own father was totally shocked by seeing her virtually naked, but he understood what had happened and admired Katie's bravery. Katie asked if she would need to wear the full hijab the next morning but the widow said if her body and head was covered that would be fine. The widow laughed and said that Katie was so pretty that the men in the village would remember her to their dying days.

Katie said how difficult it was for Ajar. The widow said she was not surprised. Initially she said her husband had been very shy. However then she laughed and said once she found out what he liked she found it easy to tell him what she found pleasurable. It was Katie's turn to laugh as she told her about Ian and what a quick learner he was. Obviously the widow knew nothing of contraception. Katie asked her, if her husband had ever had another wife. She very proudly said she always knew how to please him even when she was heavily pregnant. Katie thought, '*I'm sure I could learn a lot from this lady.*'

In the morning the daughters had great fun helping her to dress. They were fascinated by her sexy knickers which had dried over night. Katie made sure that she had their address so that she could send presents to them. She did not make the mistake of insulting them by giving them money.

The whole village turned out to see them leave. The dog took two boys to restrain him as he did not want to be parted from Katie.

They set off up the path which ran alongside the river. Katie followed behind Ajar until they were on their own. Ajar asked her to come up and walk with him, so that they could talk,

"Thank you for walking behind me out of the village." Katie smiled at him,

“I thought your stature needed a boost. It is not easy for a man who is walking with a girl who is not too bothered about wearing clothes. What is so sad is that you might have been in frenzy when you ripped them off, but it wasn’t through desire for my body. However it was the right thing to do. I would have found it difficult to swim with all that clobber on. What do you think of my clothes today? I think they are rather good and they are not hot. The widow was worried that she did not have a bra which would anywhere near fit me. So if you bide your time you may well get a glimpse of my tits. Most men enjoy having a peak.”

“Katie, I am not like most men.”

“Oh Ajar, you are, but don’t let’s argue over that. Do they think we are being followed?”

“No they don’t. They say that, although the two sides of the river are very separate, they would get word if the authorities had mounted a search.”

“That’s good news.”

“Yes but we must still be careful.”

“I will try not to strip off again!”

“Do you ever take life seriously?”

“Yes, I do, but not too often. Is there any news of the others?”

“No there was nothing, but hopefully that means like us they have reached the safety of Kurdish territory.”

“I hope we can get word to them soon as I’m worried that Ian might turn around and try to find me. Thank goodness he doesn’t realise I’m with a sex maniac who rips girls clothes off.” Ajar just did not know what to say. He held up his hands in a gesture of submission. Then they walked on in companionable silence.

In the evening Katie noticed that Ajar was breathing harder and they were walking slowly. It was not cold and so they camped out in the open. The sky was clear and there was no danger of rain. They lay down near to each other, but did not need to keep close to conserve body heat. Early in the night Ajar’s breathing became laboured and Katie became really concerned. He started coughing. She sat him up as she had been trained. This did help but she did not like his clammy skin. She started to give him sips of water being very careful not to choke him.

She guessed that he had developed pneumonia from inhaling the river water. She felt so helpless. He was too weak to walk and she was certain if she tried to carry him he would start to cough. She knew that she could run back to the village but deep down she knew they would have no medicines which would help him. She doubted that anything other than a full life support machine would save him.

She felt so empty and sad. She knew she had killed him by hitting him in the water, but if she hadn't he would have killed both of them. She decided to stay with him and just pray that he would be strong enough to survive.

At dawn he regained consciousness. She was cradling his head in her arms, as she had found that he did not cough so frequently when he was in that position. His head was on her breast. He murmured,

"Katie you are so soft. It is wrong for my head to be on your breast. Somehow I have not got the strength to resist you." Katie smiled down at him.

"I knew you had a wicked plan when you ripped my bra."

She undid the buttons of her shirt. Agar could not stop himself. He nuzzled his face between her breasts. She kissed the top of his head and tears dropped on to it. They stayed like that for several minutes. His breathing became slower. He did not regain consciousness. Poor Katie was shocked when just as he was dying, he gave three terrible gasps and then mercifully he died.

She cradled him for several more minutes before she laid him down flat.

The ground was sandy and so she dug a shallow grave. She picked some wild flowers and put them on his chest. She buried his few things including the pistol with him. After covering him with sand she spent a considerable time collecting rocks to cover him. She had not seen any wolves, but the villagers were always talking about them.

She knelt at his grave and bowed her head. Then she got up, picked up her small rucksack and set off in the direction they had planned to take.

Chapter 13

The Nomads

That evening she met a massive herd of sheep and goats down at the river. She had achieved what she had set out to do. She could now travel with these nomads North West out of Iran into Turkey always staying in areas populated by Kurds. Hopefully she could then make contact with the others.

The Nomads lived in tented camps which they moved regularly so that there was always grazing for the herds. They did have these large Iranian guard dogs, but they tended to stay in the camp and only come out with their handlers at dusk.

She was welcomed into the first encampment and shown to the leader's tent. She stood by the flap of the tent in a daze and so was not ready when she was summoned in by the leader. She knew that now was not the time to say or do anything provocative. She had noticed that she was not out of place not wearing the full hijab, but she was glad she had her head covered.

The leader was a silver haired old man who sat up straight and eyed her from top to toe. Katie felt he could almost see her body, although obviously she was properly covered. To her surprise he spoke to her in English.

"Why have you come to this part of Iran?

"I have come to find my husband who was wrongfully imprisoned in Iran and has fled here."

"It is not normal for a woman in this country to travel alone nor with a man who is not your husband. Have you been mistreated?" Katie said,

"No, I have not been mistreated. The man I was travelling with died early this morning. He had my total respect and he was entirely honourable. I buried him where we camped last night."

“Word came up the river today that an English girl swam across the river to rescue a man who was drowning. Apparently she was naked. Was that you?” Katie answered,

“Yes it was, but I was only naked, as I would have been drowned in my clothes.”

“I also heard that this girl has a power over dogs and no man would dare to touch her for fear of the dog.” Katie smiled,

“I meant no offence to your people or your religion. It is just that I am good with dogs and I’m a good swimmer.”

“That is a fair answer. Come and sit down beside me and we will talk some more.” Katie stepped forward and very delicately sat down at his feet, close beside him.

He summoned in some of his people. There was talk in Farsi. Katie gathered that they were discussing the movement of the herds who she knew were on the move, constantly seeking more grazing.

She felt herself becoming sleepy and must have leant more on to the leader’s legs. He became aware of her.

“You must be very tired. You will join my family. You don’t seem worried that I will make you a slave?” With a smile Katie replied,

“I think as a slave I would be more trouble than I’m worth, but I think as a companion you would find me good fun.” He misunderstood the good fun and said,

“Don’t worry I have three wives for that.”

“I did not mean that. I meant I love adventures and I’m sure I could make them exciting for you.”

“You mean like paddling across a very big river?”

“I think I have had enough of water for now.”

He chuckled.

“You must go to sleep. We will decide in the morning what to do with you.”

Katie was delighted how welcoming his three wives were to her. The children were fascinated by her. She was given a lovely soft bed and slept really soundly. She was surprised at herself, as she had no fear that the leader would make her into a concubine. His name was Masul and all his family seemed to love him.

She was summoned into his presence after food in the morning. Without thinking Katie leant forward and kissed him on the cheek. He laughed and said,

"That's the answer. You will be like a daughter to me. Can you ride a horse?"

"I can ride but only astride. Will I offend you if I wear trousers?" He chuckled,

"You would definitely offend everyone if you did not!"

So Katie found herself riding a spirited pony that apart from being a fidget was well behaved and did not seem to have any vices. Masul had watched her in the stables. He was amazed at how polite she was to the syces. She never used her elevated position to get her own way. She deferred to their advice.

Masul was obviously a loner as it appeared that every morning he set off on horseback on his own to go around all the large herds. Now Katie rode with him. She rode close to him but a yard behind him, always keeping to his pace. They mainly trotted, but did do some walking. They talked and they laughed. When they came to the herds, Masul would talk to the men but the children would crowd around Katie. They showed her the newborn lambs and newborn kids. Then they would set off again. Towards the middle of the day when they were in between herds, Katie saw a small copse and on impulse shouted,

"Race you to those trees!"

She set off and was soon galloping. Her head covering came off so she grabbed it in her hand. Her hair streamed behind her. Masul's horse was much bigger and stronger and slowly overhauled her pony. Masul waited at the trees as she rode up breathless and flushed. He said,

"Let us tie up the horses and sit. I have some food and water?"

Katie fumbled with her head covering. She did not want to upset him. He smiled,

"As we are alone you can just leave it. I will warn you in good time before the next herd."

As they were eating Katie suddenly became subdued. She started to think of Ian. In Tehran when he was close he was constantly in her thoughts, but now out in this marvellous countryside with all her adventures she had forgotten him. She frowned. She must try and find him. She must get him safely back to his home in Kenya. A tear ran down her cheek. Masul noticed.

"Why are you crying?" Katie sniffed

"This country is so beautiful and you and your people have been so kind. I was just remembering why I am here. I am here to free my man and take him home to Africa."

Then she told him the whole story from her arrival in Tehran. He was a good listener. Only occasionally did he interrupt for clarification. When she had finished he said,

"We will find him for you."

It was almost dark when Masul and Katie rode into the camp. Obviously there had been concern about their late arrival home. Katie was ushered away for a lovely bath. She knew she would be stiff in the morning, but the warm water was certainly a help. After supper with the female side of the family she was soon in a deep sleep. She was pleased that there was no rush in the morning as Masul was holding a council. She imagined it was from his findings about the herds and the grazing yesterday. She hoped that it might include a plan to try and locate Ian and the rest of the Kurds that had broken out of jail.

Ian knew the pistol at his head was a ruse to confuse the guards. He had become friends with the Kurds. He had regularly exercised with them. Seeing Katie had really lifted his spirits. He made a massive effort in the break time to get fit. Although it was only a small area they all made the most of it.

Now he was being dragged to the top of the mound of rubble which had once been the wall. There were two ladders on the other side and they scrambled down them as fast as they could and rushed across some open ground to two waiting vans. The Kurds urged him on and would not let him stop, let alone go back for Katie. They kept shouting,

"There is a plan for her!"

As he got into the van he saw her falling with a man off the wall, into a lorry. They slammed the door of the van and the two vans sped off through the congestion of Tehran. The two vans had obviously planned separate routes. Ian could not see where they were going.

The speed was alarming and they all were thrown around. They just clung on as best they could.

This speed paid off, as both vans unlike the lorry managed to get out of the city before the road blocks were established. They could therefore stay on the fast roads and make as quicker time as possible to the west.

The van containing Ian arrived at a lonely farm house. The van was hidden quickly under a tarpaulin in a barn. They set off in a minibus. It was only then that Ian heard about the mattresses in the lorry. Up to then he had been imagining Katie with a broken spine lying in agony in the back of a lorry. Obviously they had no idea, if the other group or Katie and Ajar had escaped but the mood was upbeat. They speeded away getting further and further from Tehran.

They spent the night north of Miyaneh in the hills. It was cold. They stayed in the minibus except when they quietly relieved themselves. They were in an old quarry about three miles from the main road. They were tempted to continue as they had plenty of fuel. However they thought the danger of them driving straight into a road block at night was too great. As dawn broke they could see normal traffic on the main road below them. They reached the main road and turned right. Soon they were on the outskirts of Tabriz. They all gave a relaxed sigh when they were safely on the other side of the city. They told Ian that the plan was for all three groups to meet up at a derelict farm, well hidden in the hills near Maku which was about twenty five miles from the Turkish border. They would then cross the border as a group during the night. They said the farm was well provisioned, but they hoped they would not have to wait too long. Every day they remained in Iran was more dangerous.

The other group had already arrived at the farm before Ian's group. The atmosphere was euphoric when they arrived. There was a big party that night.

Slowly they all started to get concerned. Where were Katie and Ajar? They all kept hidden at the farm. The local Kurds could freely travel into Maku. Obviously they could not ask a lot of questions, but there was absolutely no word about Ajar. They all began to get more and more nervous and irritable. They had a meeting. A new leader was elected. They gave Ajar three more days before they all were going to leave. Ian said nothing.

He did not know what to do. His mind was in turmoil. The sensible thing would be for him to go with the others. If Katie and Ajar had been arrested, he could get back to the UK and try and get the British Government to act. He certainly could not do anything here on the Iranian Turkish border without a passport and with very little money. However he looked on leaving as desertion. He might be a Wally at times but he was not a coward. He would never desert her. So he told the others he would stay and wait for her. They understood. It really did not concern them. They would be escaping. The local Kurds who were guarding the farm had been well paid. They knew that once the main party had left they were not really in danger. Provided they kept vigilant, if they were discovered by the authorities they could just melt into the hills. Ian could come with them or he could give himself up. So Ian had waited. All the time he became more concerned, but equally deep down inside he knew he was doing the correct thing by waiting.

They only went on a short ride that day. Katie was relieved as she was quite sore. They stopped by a lovely stream. They were totally on their own. Katie asked,

"Can I just cool my legs in the stream? My muscles are a little sore from the riding yesterday."

"Of course you can."

Masul had not been expecting anything more than Katie to get in the stream still dressed in her trousers which were more like pantaloons. Katie had other ideas. Off came her head covering and burka. Off came her pantaloons. She stepped into the stream in her knickers and a small top which covered her breasts but still showed her flat tummy. She turned calling,

"Masul, it's freezing but very therapeutic."

He was shading his eyes in horror, but he just could not resist having another look. He looked up into her laughing eyes.

"You have three lovely wives. Surely you look at them with no clothes on all the time?" He shook his head.

"No I don't. They come to me in the night. Why aren't you frightened that I will assault you?"

Katie was perplexed,

“Why would you assault me? I know you are fond of me. I think you find me attractive and amusing, but it has never occurred to me that you would assault me. I trust you with my life.” Masul answered sadly,

“I hope I can live up to that trust. Please put all your clothes back on. I just can’t think straight with you dressed in so little.”

He started to tell her how he had sent word out to all the nomads and asked them quietly to report back to him if any of them had any news of Ian and the rest of the Kurds. He said she would just have to be patient. Katie promised she would be patient and said how grateful she was to him. She said how marvellous it was for her to get out in this beautiful country. The fact that they were going west and so at least they were heading in the right direction was a great comfort to her. She said that she had not forgotten that she had broken the law in Iran and so had to be very careful that she was not arrested and get them all into trouble. They got home well before dusk. Katie was still tired and was glad to get her bed. She lay as sleep eluded her, thinking about Ian. Then she wondered which, if any, of Masul’s wives had been summoned to his bed. She wondered if he just took his pleasure or whether he enjoyed bringing his wife to ecstasy. She knew he would never ever tell her, but perhaps his wives might let on when she got to know them better.

Their daily rides continued much to Katie’s enjoyment. If they were back in good time Katie would often go and talk to the dog handlers. Soon she had the trust of both the dogs and their handlers and so she was allowed to take the dogs out for walks. Initially she only took one dog at a time but soon she was able to control several at one time.

Masul’s children started to come with her. He told her how pleased he was. He asked her if she would try to teach them English. She teased him saying,

“Of course I will, but I will make sure the girls get as good a chance as the boys.” Then she said,

“If I get them to wear suitable clothes can I teach them to swim?” He grinned,

“You can, but only if I get to check your attire first.” Katie answered,

"That is a dangerous request. I think you might have a heart attack if I get a bikini made for me." He laughed,

"What is a bikini?"

"It is two bits of cloth which will cover my breasts and my bottom."

She demonstrated with her hands on her body in a very erotic way. Masul said,

"I will get my wives to supervise. There will be no bikinis!"

The swimming and indeed the English lessons went very well. Katie was amazed how keen they were to learn. It made her smile as he often came to watch. Although she was totally covered in the water, as she came out the cloth clung to her. Thus in many ways it made her look sexier than if she had been wearing a well-fitting bikini.

They continued to go riding together. One day when they were walking close together in deep conversation, Katie became aware that there were two horsemen on the path ahead of them. She never knew what made her look quickly behind them but she was sure she glimpsed another rider. She quietly said to Masul,

"We are not alone. There is at least one rider behind us." He replied,

"I will take them on. If you get a chance, ride back the way we have come. The nearest camp is only about three miles away." Katie did not reply but just nodded her head, so he assumed she had acquiesced. In fact she was only agreeing that the camp was only three miles away. She had no intention of leaving him. She was cross with herself because she had no weapon. She wondered if he had one.

They continued to walk on together. They gave no evidence that they knew of a rider or riders behind them. Katie could see the two men that they were approaching. They both had what she knew as Len Enfield rifles. They were not automatic weapons. Masul did not stop until he was only five paces from the men. Katie guessed rightly that he had a pistol and therefore wanted to get close to them. She knew pistols are notoriously inaccurate except at close range.

She knew he must have heard the footfall of the man behind them but he gave no indication. Suddenly before the men could raise their rifles, he shot them both at point blank range in their chests. The man behind would have shot him, if Katie had not whirled her pony around and blocked the man's view. She kicked the pony in the ribs. Her reins were collected, the pony reared. One of its hooves smashed the man's skull. He was dead before his body hit the ground.

In a normal voice Katie said,

"Will there be more?"

"No I don't think so. We will ride back to that camp. They may have heard my pistol shots. They will catch the horses, and the dogs will go over the area."

He reached across and took her hand. He kissed her palm.

"You saved my life. I will never forget that. Equally I saw your hands. You totally disobeyed me. You made the pony rear. You were meant to ride off." Katie looked into his eyes,

"You must have misunderstood me. I agreed that the camp was only three miles away. I had no intention of leaving you."He smiled then.

"Iranian men beat their wives if they disobey them." With another cheeky smile Katie replied,

"I have already discussed corporal punishment with my man. Neither of us thought we would enjoy it, but I did agree that he was allowed to give my bottom a gentle squeeze. I think your wives would enjoy having their bottoms squeezed. Let me know how you get on."

Masul shook his head. She was totally beyond his understanding. He just knew that he would give his life for her.

The bandits were buried. The horses were brought into the herd and on the surface life went on as normal. However Katie did notice that there was much tighter security. Also Masul's eldest wife approached Katie when they were on their own. She said,

"Masul is a good kind man he never beats us, but he asked me if I would like him to gently squeeze my bottom. I said I thought I would enjoy it. He has never been brave enough to ask what I would enjoy before. I think you have had a very good effect on him." Katie replied,

"You must try and guide him. I think he wants all three of you to enjoy time with him."

After some days Masul told Katie that he had received news about her friends. Apparently they were still in Iran but were waiting to cross into Turkey. Masul said he imagined they were waiting for Katie and Ajar. Katie said,

"Obviously they have no idea that Ajar has died. They may think we both have been recaptured and killed. Ajar was a good man. I think he was also a good leader." Masul replied,

"They will elect a new leader and move on. They will not delay for long. I cannot decide how you can catch them up. We are relatively near to Khalkhal. They are near to Maku. That is over four hundred miles away. Let us ride and I will give the matter some thought.

They rode to another camp and then on to a small glade with a rocky stream. They were totally on their own. Katie smiled at Masul, as they sat down to eat.

"Can I tell you how strange I am?"

"Please do. I am fascinated by you and I want to understand you better."

So Katie told him about Algernon and when she had met Ian. She could see how Algernon's behaviour infuriated him. When she told him how she had forgiven Algernon and that Ian had saved his life in the hijack, he shook his head in amazement. She ended by saying,

"So I trusted Ian and then he became my man."

"So you choose him. It is very different for me as a Kurd."

"Yes I can see that. However I know you are a powerful leader and totally ruthless to your enemies, but you are a man with a great depth of feeling, particularly for women. You are going a very long way to help me. I totally trust you. I want you to be completely honest to yourself."

"I will try."

Katie started to take her clothes off in a very normal way as if she were on her own in a bathroom. He tried to turn away but he just couldn't. He watched her. When she stood before him in her knickers and small top, she said,

"It was not by chance that we came here. You know that I have to leave you and you wanted to see me one more time. Am I right?"

He nodded his head. Katie continued,

"I think your wives would enjoy it if you brought them to beautiful places like this. I think they would really enjoy you making love to them slowly and gently not only in the dark but also in the light."

Then she started to cry, saying thro her tears,

"If I did not have a man, you would be on the top of my list."

Masul handed up her clothes to her.

"I will return you to your man"

As they rode in the afternoon he told her his plan.

In the camp was a lorry which was used to move the baggage when they moved camp. It also was used to transport sheep and goats when they were ready to go to the abattoir. It was modified by Masul's men. In the middle of the lower deck they constructed a wooded box which was big enough for Katie to sit in and even to lie down in. Sheep and goats were free to walk all around it. It was attached to the top deck so the animals could walk on top of it. Katie would be able to get out of it through a trap door in the deck. She would then be with the sheep and goats on the upper deck and could get out of the truck by climbing over the high sides. Although Katie tried to reason with him, Masul insisted he would come with two of his men the following morning to take some stock through Tabriz to Maku. They would leave at 2 am to get through Tabriz before the place got busy

Katie did not need to be woken. She had got her bag together with her proper clothes the night before. She was dressed only in a little dress. She kissed the sleeping children and Masul's three wives. She got into her box. The sheep and goats were quickly loaded and they were off. She was not that uncomfortable as she had blankets and cushions, together with plenty of water and food. She knew she would just be very bored.

After six hours the lorry turned off the main road. It carried on for two miles to a lonely place on a small river. Masul made sure they were not overlooked before the men let the stock off for a drink. Katie hopped out and quickly went to the loo before having a quick swim in the river. Then she ran to him in her wet dress and whispered in his ear,

"I'm surprised you haven't stopped several times before."

"I've been very tempted."

They set off after the animals had drunk and been loaded again. It was now quite warm so Katie took off her dress and hung it up to dry in her box. She lay down in the nude on the cushions and blankets, and went to sleep. She woke, as she felt the lorry slowing down. She just lay there. She guessed it was a road block. She did not want to move in case she made a noise or disturbed the animals. However her worries were unfounded and they were soon moving again. It had been a road block but the police were not suspicious.

She did not sleep again and so she felt another turn off the main road. She put her dress back on. She could hear the different tone of the lorry and knew they were climbing. Slowly it got colder so she wrapped herself in the blankets. She ate some food, so that she was ready if she had to get out quickly.

It was almost dark when they stopped. Katie was already in her burka and got out as Masul opened the trap door. Before he could leave her she wrapped her arms around him and kissed his cheek. She felt his hands on her bottom. He said,

"Somehow I could not stop them."

"I'm glad you couldn't. I wish you Godspeed and thank you." He clambered down the side of the truck and caught her as she jumped. No more was said. She saw a man in the shadows and walked towards him. He just turned and set off uphill on a narrow path. She followed him. She heard the lorry turning and then it set off in the opposite direction. She was not nervous but was very excited. She felt she must be getting nearer to Ian and hopefully freedom for both of them.

They kept walking without a break for four hours. Katie was fit but the altitude was beginning to take its toll, when they stopped by a small stream. They both drank and after ten minutes they set off again. The next two hours were gruelling for Katie. She was almost on her knees when she sensed the presence of another man. She slumped to the ground. There was a whispered conversation. The new man whispered to her,

"You have done well. Have a short rest. You have only twenty minutes to go now."

Katie trudged on after the man.

Chapter 14

At last they meet again

The farm was well hidden and they had arrived before Katie realised. She followed the man into the dwelling. There were no lights but Katie could make out some camp beds. Only one was occupied. The body stirred. It was Ian. She just stood in a state of shock. She had made it. He had waited for her. She leant down and kissed his cheek. He was immediately awake,

"Katie, my darling girl." His arms were around her and she burst into tears with relief. They were oblivious to the other man who went out to continue his guard duty. They were too emotional to speak. They sat together on the bed with their arms around each other. Then Ian lay down on his back drawing Katie on top of him. He stroked her hair.

"I never want to leave you again. Will you marry me?"

"I have been a naughty girl."

"I don't care how naughty you have been. I love your naughty ways." Katie's confidence deserted her. She snivelled and wiped her nose on his neck. She whispered,

"I hoped you would ask so I married you in your absence. It will make it easier for us to get home. I have a passport in the name of Mrs. Richardson in my bag. Are you annoyed?" She heard his soft laugh.

"I'm delighted. Falling asleep with my face in your crutch was the best thing I ever did." Katie retorted,

"What you did in my crutch had nothing to do with it!" Then she felt his hand. She managed to say,

"You bugger." Then they were pulling their clothes off.

They slept a little but they woke with the dawn. They knew there was no rush as they had until dusk before they had to attempt the crossing into Turkey. They had breakfast with the local Kurds who were not really guarding them but were acting as caretakers. One called Jamal elected to lead them that night. Katie cried when she told him about how Ajar had died.

Then Katie questioned him carefully, as she realised that if the climb and the trip were as hard as the journey was yesterday, she would struggle to make it. Jamal encouraged her saying it was not so hard. He had a smirk on his face when he suggested they made use of the day to have real physical rest and proper sleep. Katie laughed,

"I'm sorry about last night." He replied,

"I think they could probably have heard you in Tehran."

So when Katie and Ian had finished breakfast they lay down in separate beds and slept. Ian woke in the early afternoon and quietly went out without waking Katie. He packed his bag, discarding as much as he could. He was amazed that Katie had so little but he packed it in his bag. He resisted the urge to look at the passports. He knew she would show him in her own good time.

Katie woke in time to have the communal meal and then there was lots of goodbyes before Jamal led them out of the valley. As far as they all knew the others had made it safely across the border. They were sure they would have heard, as the others had left two weeks earlier. Katie was so grateful to Ian for waiting for her.

Initially they made good time, but when it got really dark their speed lessened. What Katie found annoying was that it was just as tiring going slowly, picking their way in the dark. They did not dare to use a torch.

Soon after 11.00 pm the moon started to rise. Their speed increased. Also they were now on a wide plateau so there was less climbing. Katie was well aware how disastrous it would be if she slipped and twisted an ankle. She steadily followed Jamal and Ian was right behind her. She mused, '*All her tottering about on high heels may have strengthened her leg muscles.*' Ever the realist she thought, '*I think it only makes my bottom bigger. Maybe that had been for the best, as when she had been such a fool as to suggest to Ian that he pulled her knickers down, the delay getting them over her bottom may have saved the day! She so loved him. She stiffened her resolve and kept pace with Jamal.*'

They stopped for a break when they were above Gorik. Katie knew that this was the most dangerous section of the trip. They had to descend into a valley and cross a relatively major road which ran north from Maku to Ararat. They could see the road in the moonlight. There were very few vehicles, but she was aware that if they were seen by a police vehicle they would be in trouble. After the rest, they descended. This in itself was more hazardous as going down increased the chance of turning an ankle.

There were bushes on both sides of the road which helped them. Jamal had said that the big group had planned to cross singly, but over supper he had said that, as there were only three of them, he thought the safest thing was for them to cross all together. A truck came by and they all lay on the ground averting their eyes to preserve their night vision. Katie was thankful that it was dry. As soon as it had passed Jamal gave the signal and they sprinted across. No further vehicles came and they steadily climbed out of the valley. Katie was so grateful to Jamal. Without him, she and Ian would not have made it.

Suddenly Jamal stopped and Katie managed to stop without cannoning into him. Mercifully Ian was not that close and so he stopped without making a noise. Katie could then hear the sound of several pairs of army boots. Jamal beckoned her to follow him, as he moved left off the path. Ian followed her. There were voices and she could see torches. She remembered Southern Ethiopia. If only there were some big baobabs. There was nothing here except this fairly thin bush. Jamal indicated for them to lie down. The patrol got nearer. Katie prayed that they would not use their torches to search the sides of the path. She saw a soldier almost tread on Ian.

They lay for about twenty minutes before Jamal let them continue on their way. He whispered to Katie,

"They were Turks. We have crossed the border. We will continue to Ciftlik. We can lodge with a friend of mine as we have been a little slow. You will have to delay getting to Dogubayazit for another day."

It was almost day break when they arrived in Ciftlik. Jamal's friend was actually Jamal's Uncle. They were ushered inside quickly. Jamal's Uncle was very welcoming, but he was obviously worried about Katie, as the hut was very basic. They sat around his table and were given tea and a type of cake which tasted of lemon.

Jamal's Uncle had not seen them, but apparently the big group had got through without a hitch. He was sorry to hear about Ajar.

When Katie gave an abridged version of the river crossing, Jamal's Uncle looked even more worried. He said,

"You have to cross the Rud-e-Zangemir. It is a very dangerous river. Katie got Jamal to translate and explain that she and Ian were both very good swimmers. She said sadly it was Ajar who was not a good swimmer.

Although they were now in Turkey, they were by no means safe. They had entered illegally and the Turks might just send them back into Iran with disastrous consequences. Jamal said he would show them the river tomorrow and then they would have to decide how they were going to proceed from there. His job was finished and he would return to Iran on the following night.

Katie and Ian were ready to go to bed. Jamal's Uncle was worried about the small single bed. He had been told that Katie and Ian were married. It was while there were discussions about the bed that Katie got out the two British Passports that Sir Alan had sent to her. As she thumbed through the pages she saw that Sir Alan had had them stamped as if they had legally left Iran and had also legally entered Turkey. This was marvellous, as she now remembered all that time ago in London with Raymond Hadfield that he was going to leave airline tickets in an envelope in their names in the 'Sultan Hotel' in Dogubayazit. Katie decided to keep her passport in her maiden name, as that would be a relatively normal thing to do. However she burnt the forged Iranian passports, as they would still be incriminating either back in Iran or here in Turkey.

Katie and Ian cuddled up together and slept. They were totally exhausted.

May be it was the memory of Ajar as Katie found the sight of the river very daunting. Ian had no such worries and so did his best to encourage her. They both decided that they would make the attempt that day as if they stayed it increased their risk of discovery. Although Jamal offered to try and find a boat, he did not sound hopeful and once again going anywhere near a village would put them all in danger.

They were totally on their own and so to Jamal's surprise without further discussion, they both took off all their clothes.

Ian said,

"Katie you are so marvellous."

"Ian, I love you. You are so predictable. You always praise me when you want sex or when you expect me to do something dangerous. Which is it now?"

Ian gave her a rather sad look. She continued with a grin,

"I will be fine crossing the river. As a new loyal wife I will expect some sex on the other side."

They packed the clothes into several polythene bags, before putting them in the rucksack. Ian strapped it securely on his back. In the nude they shook hands with a totally bemused Jamal and holding hands carefully climbed down the bank into the river.

They had packed their tackies as they could see the bank was mainly sand with smooth boulders. Jamal stood and watched them. Initially they made good progress going straight over the river. Then the current started to pull them down stream. They didn't fight it but continued swimming steadily. Jamal became really alarmed for their safety when they hit the turbulence of the main current. He could hardly see them. At one point he was sure that they had drowned, but at last he could see them in calmer water on the other side of the turbulent middle stream.

He was so relieved. As he was in no hurry he walked down the bank so that he was level with them as they emerged from the water. He just could not believe his eyes. The woman lay on her back on the sand only just out of the water. She drew the man who still had the rucksack on his back on top of her and they made love. He ran back to his Uncle's house. What a story he had to tell.

Ian lay on top of her panting. She laughed,

"As a shag that was bloody useless, but I am a dutiful wife and I just lay on my back and thought of England! However I will be expecting considerable improvements. Kenya is such a beautiful country. I think I will think about Kenya in future while you are performing."

Ian kissed her saying,

"I'm sorry, am I that hopeless?" She answered,

"Yes but I will forgive you. You are a good swimmer. Come on let's get to civilization. You can always get better and I do admit that you are out of practice. At least I hope you are out of practice!"

They got dressed. They were now English tourists, but Katie was well covered up, as she did not want to, either draw attention to herself, or to upset the local people. She was pleased as they often held hands and Ian took every opportunity to put his hand on her thigh.

It was a long walk into Dogubayazit, but the sun was shining and so they chatted about their experiences. They saw very few people, but those they did smiled and said a few words. Katie was sorry that she did not know any Turkish.

She told Ian all about Ajar. It helped her to grieve as she had grown fond of him. When she talked about Masul, Ian guessed that she had found him very attractive. Katie was totally open,

"I did really fancy him. He was very kind and I suppose the fact that he was so powerful influenced my judgement a little." Then with a laugh she added,

"However I was a married woman and I took my responsibilities very seriously!"

Then she wrapped herself around him and they kissed passionately. When they broke apart she said,

"Well you won't have to content with a bossy Miss. KK anymore. You will have to put up with a nagging Mrs. KR. My advice is that you remember to kiss her like that as often as possible."

They walked on holding hands with smiles on their faces.

Dogubayazit was not a large town and they easily found the 'Sultan Hotel'. To their delight the envelope with their open airline tickets was handed over. They checked in and were told that it would be quite OK for them to settle the hotel bill in dollars. The receptionist took their passports for inspection by the police. As they were a married couple they only had to complete one registration form. Katie whispered to Ian,

"At least being married has one advantage."

They went into the restaurant. They had cokes to drink. There really were only two choices of food; fish or meat. Katie had not appetite for fish. In fact she was sure they both smelt distinctly fishy. She just hoped that they would not appear distinctly fishy to the authorities. It was now evening and so they were ready to go to bed. However they went to the receptionist and enquired about flights.

Apparently there was only one a day for Istanbul which left at 11.00 am. He was happy to reserve them a place.

When they got to the room, they both suddenly were shy. Katie regretted teasing Ian,

"I'm sorry I teased you my darling. Somehow I just can't seem to be natural." He put his arms around her and kissed her gently.

"That's a good start." Then the Katie of old, said,

"We will have to do something about your '*mkia*'. It will be like trying to stuff a marshmallow into a letterbox." Ian laughed,

"You have no idea how much I have missed you. I was seriously missing you before the DVS even sent me to Iran."

"Would you like me to leave BOAC and join East African Airways and do short-haul?"

"It would not be nearly so glamorous?"

"May be not, but I think going on safari with you would definitely make up for the lack of glamour."

She put her hand down to him saying,

"Well your '*mkia*' certainly agrees. I now feel sexy. Look out Richardson you are back with a she-cat. Forget about this wife malarkey!"

Morning came all too soon. They were surprised as they boarded on to the plane early and took off on time. They were given a cup of very thick black coffee and a glass of water, together with a sickly piece of cake. Ian whispered to Katie,

"Is all short-haul food as bad as this? You will waste away. I will have to get Nelson to feed you up."

"Do you think I'm too thin?" Ian put his hand on her thigh and gave it a gentle squeeze,

"You are just right." She put her hand on his and quickly kissed his neck, only to find the pretty air hostess looking down at them. Katie whispered to her,

"Sorry that was very naughty I did not want to offend you, but we are on honeymoon." The air hostess smiled and walked on. Ian whispered,

"She is thinking, however has a beautiful young girl like her ended up with an ugly old codger like him?" With a cheeky grin Katie said,

“There can only be one of two reasons, either you are filthy rich or you are very good in bed. Last night was good fun!”

They only had hand luggage and so connecting to their Nairobi flight with East African Airways in Istanbul was no problem. It was almost empty and so Katie had a chat with the senior air hostess. She said that Katie would have no problem getting a job as they were desperately short of trained cabin staff on short-haul. Katie made her laugh as when the air hostess said the only bad thing about East African Airways were the pilots who were not the sharpest tools in the shed. Katie said, “This one is a Private Pilot. You want to try flying with him. When I took all my clothes off to join the ‘Mile High Club’ he thought I must be too hot and opened the cabin air-vent!” When she had stopped laughing the young lady suggested that perhaps it would be best if Katie did not mention that qualification on her CV.

As they were getting off the plane in the morning, the air hostess said, handing Katie a piece of paper,

“Do contact me if I can help you to get a job.” Then looking at Ian she whispered,

“Was it fun?” Katie replied,

“It was certainly most memorable.”

They were both excited as they left the terminal. Ian had a broad grin on his face as he commandeered a taxi to take them to Kabete. They both chatted to the driver in Swahili as if they were old friends of his.

When they arrived at Ian’s house, swept Katie off her feet to carry her over the threshold. He was holding her in his arms, as Nelson came out to greet them. He asked in Swahili if they were well and if they had been on a good safari. Ian replied traditionally, saying they were both very well and had been on a very good safari. Then Ian added that they had got married. Nelson gave them a very rare smile saying,

“It will take me a little time to make supper. Would they like to make a baby while they waited?”

They did their best!